SUVI'S REVENGE

DARK WARRIOR ALLIANCE BOOK 6

BRENDA TRIM
TAMI JULKA

UNTITLED

Copyright © 2015 by Brenda Trim and Tami Julka

Editor: Amanda Fitzpatrick
Cover Art by Patricia Schmitt (Pickyme)

As summer comes to an end we are faced with major changes in our children's lives. Tami's oldest son, Torrey, enlisted in the Marines and her youngest, Nick, is starting the seventh grade. Brenda's oldest, Maddie, is a senior in high school, her son, Keegan, is going into the fifth grade and her youngest, Izzy, is starting the third grade. Our time with them has been and always will be priceless. We love them to the moon and back.

As always, we want to say a heartfelt thank you to all of our readers! We are thrilled that you have embraced our young, energetic witches and if you're sad that their stories have come to an end, be sure to check out our Dark Warrior Alliance series, if you haven't already. We have fierce dragons, angels bent on vengeance and more demons coming your way!

CHAPTER 1

"I didn't fucking do this! I *am* innocent," Caine DuBray slammed his fists on the table and looked Zander, his vampire king, in the eyes. He took several deep breaths to calm down. Disrespecting his king would only have beheaded head that much sooner. It was all still so surreal and he couldn't believe the mess he was in. He had been casually dating a human named Sally for several months, and the image of her lying lifeless with her throat ripped out was imbedded in his brain. Her skin had been a sickly shade of grey, telling him that she had been drained of blood.

"I cared for her, I would never hurt her. Or any female for that matter, it goes against everything I am." In fact, his father would tan his hide if he ever dreamed of it. He may be an adult but Ellis DuBray wouldn't hesitate to beat him senseless for disrespecting any female. Besides, he would never risk suffering the consequence for such an act.

Caine gritted his teeth as his eyes roamed the large conference room in the famed Zeum compound. He had fantasized about seeing the inside of the mansion and he couldn't believe he was finally there. However, in his dreams, he was there because the king had asked for his help with the Vampire Nation's finances. Even in his worst nightmares, he would never have been there under such shitty circumstances. The rich, wood floors and the high, coffered ceilings may be elegant and immense, but at the moment, they were closing in on him.

Zander pinned him with a hard stare. He felt the power of compulsion coming off his leader in waves. The sharp sting of the force almost had him wincing and lowering his head, but he held his position. He needed Zander to see that he was telling the truth. Not for a moment did he fear Zander would see anything to implicate him.

Zander sighed and placed his hands on the table, clasping them together. His exasperation was obvious. Zander cared about his subjects, but to see his upset over this drove that point home. He'd grown up hearing stories how Zander had been the saving grace for the realm. The development of the Dark Alliance and the Dark Warriors had been nothing short of genius in protecting the humans and realm members.

"All the evidence points to you, Caine. You must see how bad this looks. You were found passed oot in her home, seemingly from draining the puir lass dry. The human authorities were called and you are lucky that Orlando and Santiago arrived at the scene first and sensed your presence. Shite," the king raked his hands through his hair, disheveling his shoulder-length black strands. "Had they no' removed you from the home it would have been all over the media. The Tehrex Realm could have verra likely been exposed by this." The more agitated the King became, the thicker his Scottish accent became.

"I swear to you, Liege, the last thing I remember is going to her house. We had opened a bottle of wine and were talking on her couch and then...nothing. I have no recollection of anything after that. The next thing I knew, I woke up here in the dungeons thirty minutes ago. I swear to you, I did not kill Sally. I know it sounds crazy and I have no idea who would have done it, but I think I was drugged. My head hurts, my stomach is upset, and I'm parched. There is no reason for me to have these symptoms. Test my blood and see what you find." Vampires were immune to human illnesses and when they had symptoms like these it typically indicated drugs or heavy alcohol use.

Zander had to believe him. He wasn't ready for his life to end yet. He had too much he still wanted to do. Caine felt as if his body was coiled so tight he may fracture from the tension and had no idea how to relieve it. Nothing in his life had prepared him for a situation like this. He had great parents who loved him and a good job making decent money. Banking wasn't fraught with life-and-death possibilities in the Tehrex Realm.

"You could be feeling like this because you did the forbidden and killed while you fed, ending up in a blood-induced black-out." Zander snarled as he stood up, his black combat boots echoing loudly as the large male crossed to a long table at the back wall that held several computers and telephones. The king was intimidating even with his back to him. He wore black from head to toe and strength coiled in the ropes of the muscles covering his body, but it was the power that emanated from the king that grated across Caine's nerves like razors. He didn't doubt that Zander could pop his head from his shoulders without breaking a sweat.

Caine's stomach knotted up when the king picked up the phone. "Jace, I need you to come down to the war room.

And, bring your medical bag." Caine held back his relief at the thought that maybe Zander believed him. He wasn't going to allow himself any hope until he had something firm to grasp onto. Still, it was a good sign that he was asking the Dark Warrior's healer to come down.

The king replaced the receiver on the cradle and turned back to face Caine. The leader of vampires and Dark Warriors sat on the edge of the table, bracing his weight with his hands. "Here is what's going to happen. Jace is going to take your blood. Och, speak of the devil. Jace, you are aware of the situation regarding Caine. He believes that he has been drugged. Take his blood and analyze it for everything. Doona leave any possibility oot. This matter is far too serious."

Caine was sweating and his heart raced with fear, but maybe there was a way out of this nightmare. "Thank you, Liege," he replied, genuflecting before Jace approached him.

"Have a seat, Caine. You are shaking far too much for me to do this while you are standing. It won't take long." Caine didn't know why he was shaking so badly. Even if he had no memory of the evening, he knew deep down he was innocent. Jace pulled out a chair and Caine sank into it, allowing some of the tension to leave his shoulders. He rolled up his sleeve for him to draw the blood as the Dark Warrior opened a bag and placed several tubes and a needle on the table.

Zander's voice brought his attention away from what Jace was doing and his words had the tension returning tenfold. "That willna be enough to prove your innocence. It may prove that you were under the influence but that doesna mean anything. You could have taken drugs of your own accord, after all. We need more proof than that or you will face the sentence. My hands are tied." Zander spread his arms, palms up and shrugged his shoulders. It was clear the king wanted to believe he wasn't responsible, but there was only so much he could do. Just the fact that he had allowed him to voice his position spoke volumes about Zander.

It was one thing to be given the chance to prove his innocence, but he had no idea how he was going to go about it. Zander was right. The circumstantial evidence was damning and there were no witnesses he could call on. The only other person that had been in the house was dead. Caine's gut dropped to the floor and he was having difficulty breathing. This couldn't be happening. It was a nightmare that would never end. "How much time do I have?" Jace withdrew the needle and swiped the drop of blood that escaped before his natural healing took care of the wound.

Zander glanced down and pinched his forehead with his thumb and first finger. "I can give you seventy-two hours. No more." He looked up then and Caine saw the regret and sorrow in his blue eyes. "Jace will place a tracker under your forearm that will allow us to know where you are at all times. If you try to remove it, it will kill you. It will also compel you to return for sentencing at the end of that time."

As a full-blown panic attack struck him, Caine hardly felt Jace implant the device. His head was swimming, he couldn't draw a breath, was sweating profusely and his pulse was racing as if it could escape this reality. "Seventy-two hours isn't enough time. You know I really only have half that amount of time, since I can't go out during the day. What am I supposed to do?"

Jace placed a compassionate hand on his shoulder and drew his attention. He found it difficult to focus on what the

Dark Warrior was saying and had to shake his head to clear the fog. "Only magic will be able to solve this mystery. I suggest going to the Rowan sisters. They helped me with a rather ugly situation and they've helped many others in the realm, as well. In fact, if rumor is to be believed, they are next in line for Wiccan leadership. Anyway, it hurts nothing to ask and they can investigate during the daylight hours."

Zander walked into his line of sight. "Jace is right. They are a valuable resource. They have a shop downtown, Black Moon Sabbat. Bring me that evidence, Caine. You have seventy-two hours or I will be forced to put you to death."

"Oooh, look at this silver Druzy. I bet it sparkles in the sunlight. I love it. I'm keeping this one for me, it matches the color of my shoes perfectly," Suvi yelped excitedly as she and her two sisters unpacked their replacement shipment from RockCandy Leatherworks. She'd bet that they were Shannon's best customer given that they'd had to place an extensive order twice in less than a month. Between the car bomb and the skirmish with Cele, their store had seen its share of destruction.

"You're right. I never thought there would be a stone that sparkled as much as those shoes, but it does," her sister Pema added. She heard the incredulity in her sister's tone. Pema was the oldest of the triplets and by far the most practical.

"You should call your BF Plain Paula and see how many calories you would burn running around in those six-inch stilettos," Isis, the middle sister said, laughing. Suvi joined her laughter and soon all three of them were crying from laughing so hard. Plain Paula was a running joke between her and her sisters. The female was beyond annoying with her constant lectures about fitness.

Suvi sobered and glanced around their shop. Only with the help of Isis' mate, Braeden, had they been able to make as much progress, and in such a short amount of time, in repairing the shop. She was glad to see it finally open for business after the explosion that resulted from their magic colliding with Cele's. That incident had been the second time in weeks that the shop had been destroyed. The first time, it had been Cele's daughter who had attempted to kill Pema by planting a bomb in her car that was right outside their shop. In short, they may have lost everything, but it was replaceable. What mattered most was they hadn't lost their lives.

Suvi watched Ronan and Braeden, her sisters' mates, roll their eyes at the gushing that was going on over the interchangeable stones for the jewelry they carried. Pema and Isis had gone back to unpacking while Suvi mused at how much their lives had changed in the past few weeks. Pema had found her mate, a bear shifter with a penchant for growling, and now Isis had her mate who brought his son. To say that their house was full was an understatement, but Suvi wouldn't have it any other way.

"Don't you have enough stones? And, aren't you supposed to be selling those?" Ronan asked Pema with a husky laugh as he crossed to her side and crushed her in an embrace. Suvi sighed at the sight. It was terribly romantic to watch them. They adored each other and couldn't seem keep their hands off one another.

Isis and her mate, Braeden, were also madly in love, but they didn't express it as openly. Theirs was a stolen touch, followed by a heated gaze, probably because it was difficult for them to be more openly affectionate with Donovan around. The stripling had been through an ordeal, almost dying at the hands of Cele, and needed constant reassurance from his father and his new mother that he was safe and no one was going to hurt him again. They all doted on the stripling. It was hard not to love him with his curly, brown hair and big, blue eyes that would steal anyone's heart.

Donovan dropped the bags of tea and began jumping up and down, waving his tiny, little arm in the air. "Aunt Suvi always says that females can never have too many jewels. Don't you know that, Uncle Ronan? Kids too. I love the Lil' Rock that Shannon made me," he squealed, holding his wrist out for everyone to see the leather strap with a black, onyx stone. Suvi couldn't help but ruffle his hair and smile.

"You are correct, little one. And, don't ever forget that, either. The grumpy, old bear still doesn't get it. What has Auntie Suvi told you about that?"

"That I must shower my mate with love and affection and lots of jewelry and shoes. Oh, and all that growling I hear is really just Uncle Ronan play-wrestling with Aunt Pema," Donovan responded. Suvi winked at her sister and her mate. Too many times she'd had to entertain the boy and explain what the noise was. No doubt his budding cambion senses understood the truth on some level.

"Is that what my dad and mom were doing the night of their mating ceremony?" he asked innocently. It warmed Suvi's heart to hear him calling Isis mom. She had worried that it would be difficult for him to embrace her sister given his loyalty to his birth mother. Not, in Suvi's opinion, that the female deserved his allegiance in any way when she abandoned the boy as a baby and hadn't tried to contact him even once.

Isis choked out a laugh. "Well, Donovan. What your dad

and I did was...uh," Isis faltered and Braeden came to her rescue.

"We were completing our mating, son. You know there are many steps to cementing our union and earning the Goddess' blessing. The ceremony is a public part and the blood exchange is private."

"The best part was seeing the magic that made mom's stone grow into her palm. It was cool," he said grabbing Isis' hand to look at the sapphire embedded into her sister's palm. Suvi considered the chocolate diamond in Pema's palm and looked down at her own, empty one, wondering when she'd find her Fated Mate and what color hers would be.

"You're right. It was very cool," Braeden agreed.

"Will my mate's stone do the same thing? Because I think that would be awesome," Donovan asked as he danced around the store, trampling bubble wrap as he went.

Braeden stopped him and tickled Donovan's tummy. "No one knows what the Goddess has in store for you. If you're lucky you will find someone as wonderful as Isis."

"I hope so. Hey, does this mean I'm going to have a little sister or brother soon?" Suvi laughed at the way Isis paled. She doubted her sister would be ready for a child for a while yet.

The tinkling of the new chimes above their door startled her and interrupted the conversation. She hadn't gotten used to their new sound yet, the metal's tone was much harsher, but served its purpose. She turned around and felt the breath leave her body in one great exhale.

A God stood before her. A male, well over six feet tall with a firmly muscled body, took up the entrance. He wasn't like most supernatural males, either. Most were rugged and casual, preferring jeans and t-shirts. There were the exceptions and this male was one hell of an exception in his black, two-piece suit that was tailored to his sculpted body like a work of art. His shaggy, black hair didn't fit his attire as disheveled as it was, falling into his green eyes.

The sensation of electricity rippling through her veins stunned Suvi. There was always a rush when she practiced magic, but this was so much more than that. She was captured by his gaze and her entire being woke to pay attention. She noticed the haggard look on his face as he loosened his blue pin-striped tie, walking into the store. The way he moved reminded her of a panther and she wanted desperately to be his prey.

"What's wrong with Suvi, daddy?" She heard Donovan ask followed by Braeden's chuckle.

"You'll understand some day, son. Come on. Let's go get some ice cream down the street." She heard the door sound again when Braeden and Donovan left, but she didn't move. She couldn't. She was rooted to the spot.

Caught in an erotic trance, Suvi became aware that she was gawking. In her defense, any female would be in this male's presence. The touch of her sister's hand on her shoulder brought her out of her apodyopsis, and she blushed with embarrassment.

"Are you the Rowan sisters?" The somber note to his deep voice had Suvi doing a double take and that's when she noted the haunted look to his gorgeous, green eyes. She wondered what put that look there, and oddly, she wanted to put a smile on his face and make that expression disappear.

Pema extended her hand. "Yes, we are. I'm Pema and these are my sisters, Isis and Suvi," she pointed to them in turn. "How can we help you?" Suvi noticed how Ronan had abandoned hanging shelves and come to stand directly behind Pema.

"I'm not sure where to begin and I don't even know if you can help me." He seemed nervous and out of sorts and Suvi felt compelled to promise him she'd move heaven and earth to help him. "I'm Caine DuBray. Jace and Zander thought maybe you three could help me with a situation that I have suddenly found myself in. It's a nightmare, really." He paused and placed his hands in his pockets. She saw the muscles flex in his neck from clenching his jaw tightly.

Suvi was inexplicably drawn to him and overcome with a fierce need to erase the shadows. She wanted to draw him into her arms and hold him tightly. She knew what would put a smile on his face and she was all too happy to volunteer. Not that she was being entirely selfless given that she was pretty sure it would put a smile on hers, too.

She placed her hand on his forearm, unsure when her feet had carried her to his side. The feel of the soft fabric under her palm disappeared when another electrical charge lit her up. His eyes widened and he stared at her, clearly feeling the same thing. She found her voice after several silent seconds. "We will help you. I promise. We haven't been dubbed the prophesized triplets for nothing."

"Hold up, Suvi. Let's hear what he needs help with before you go promising the moon," Isis chided. Suvi quickly rounded on her sister, glaring daggers. Isis had her happy-ever-after and Suvi just wanted a few minutes with this magnificent male so her sister needed to back the hell off.

"Isis," Suvi growled.

"No, Suvi," Isis countered and the lights in the store flickered from the increase of emotion she was absorbing. Suvi didn't care right then if Isis' anger caused an earthquake and swallowed their store. Suvi was startled when she felt warm hands on her shoulders and turned her head, falling into his deep, green orbs once again.

"Please, your sister is right. You need to hear what I ask and consider it carefully before you decide. I have been framed for a crime and face death." Suvi listened raptly as he retold the situation he awoke to earlier that evening. In her soul, she knew that this vampire was innocent just as surely as she knew she and her sisters could do something about it. The fact that Zander had sent him to them reinforced her belief. She rubbed at her chest when an unfamiliar twisting took her breath.

She grabbed her sisters' hands. "I know we have Cele to deal with, but we are the only ones who can do this. We can't let him die," she implored.

"This will be dangerous," Ronan rumbled.

Suvi whirled around, anger blazing through her. "Of course it will be dangerous, you oaf, but if it were Pema you would do whatever it took. Just because he isn't in your little circle of friends, doesn't mean he isn't worth the risk." She was shaking with fierce emotion, and at that moment, knew she'd do this, with or without her sisters, although it would be much easier with them.

Two things happened simultaneously. Caine grabbed onto her shoulders and Pema jumped in before the situation deteriorated more. "Suvi. Of course we will do what we can. However, our priority must be on dealing with the threat Cele presents to us if we happen to find her."

"He only has seventy-two hours," Suvi all but wailed.

Caine stepped into her and cupped her cheek, awe written all over his face. "Suvi, stop and think about this. Your sister is right. You can't allow a threat against you to go unanswered."

She was once again caught in his thrall. She wished she understood why he held such power over her. It wasn't like she was unfamiliar with good-looking males. "Why would that be more important than saving your life?"

The smile Caine gave her held the world and she wanted to live in it.

CHAPTER 2

Caine could not believe his luck. The worst day of his life just turned into the absolute best day of his life. And, the reality was that it may actually be one of his last. If it was, at least he had one of the hottest females he'd ever seen in his corner. The infamous Rowan triplets had brought him back to their house and if he wasn't misreading Suvi's body language, she wanted him. He wasn't going to say no to the sexy witch. He may only have three days to live and he planned on grabbing life by the balls.

He glanced around the backyard, impressed that the three sisters had done so well for themselves at such a young age. Supernaturals didn't mature out of their stripling years and into adulthood until they turned twenty-five and the triplets were only twenty-seven. They were impressive, indeed.

He squinted at the tiny lights that seemed to be floating around the shrubbery. Fireflies immediately came to mind, but they weren't indigenous to Seattle. Upon closer inspection, he realized they were bigger than a firefly, as well. He noticed that there were flowers all around their property despite it being a chilly, fall night. Typically, by that time of the year, the flowers were done blooming and the leaves had turned colors.

One of the lights zoomed past his face and he instinctively swatted at it. Dodging his hand, the object moved closer to him and buzzing sounded in his ear. He turned his head to see what it was and focused on a tiny, winged female hovering in front of him.

It was then that he realized that the lights were Fae creatures called sprites. Sprites were Unseelie and some of the most delicate, yet powerful, beings in the Fae realm. To earn their allegiance was difficult, even for the Unseelie King. He understood the flowers when he saw the tiny faerie. They likely tended the witches' gardens and ensured there were flowers year round. He smiled and lifted a finger and the smallest hand he'd ever seen closed around the end of it.

"Hi there. You're beautiful," he told the little being with her long, blonde hair and big, green eyes. She wore a layered dress made of iridescent fabric that was a shade darker than her wings. Her bare feet hung in the air and he had the urge to tickle them. She smiled at his compliment, then quickly turned and flew away.

He laughed and glanced around, watching the show. The sprites were dancing and playing with one another before the magical backdrop of Lake Washington. The lush greenery that surrounded the large pool made more sense to him now. He wondered how Suvi and her sisters had earned the loyalty of so many sprites. It told him much about their character.

He took off his jacket and tossed it over one of the chairs and considered how lucky he was to have their help. His tie followed suit as he thought of the hot, little witch. He could tell that Suvi was a bundle of fun. In her impossibly high heels and her sensual beauty, she exuded sex appeal. He imagined males everywhere threw themselves at her and he wasn't ashamed to admit he was willing to join their ranks.

The way her eyes had glowed with heated passion while she pleaded his case warmed his aching heart. And when his eyes had been drawn to her legs in her short skirt, he almost lost it. Those shoes of hers only accentuated her calf muscles, making his mouth water. She moved with an innate grace that exceeded what was common for supernaturals.

Speak of the siren. He focused on her silhouette as she sauntered out the back door. His cock went hard at the sight of her long, creamy legs and soft, flat abdomen, and full breasts bouncing as she walked. She wore another pair of high heels and a skimpy, neon-orange bikini. Her silky, black hair flowed loose and long down her back and he wanted to grab a fist of it. His vision became tinged with green, telling him they were glowing with his arousal and her brown eyes glowed brightly, mirroring his reaction. He silently thanked the Goddess for creating such a sexy creature.

He took a deep breath and caught tendrils of her succulent melon scent that was teasing his nostrils. The scent reminded him of summertime and sunshine. The association was odd for a vampire, given that they couldn't be out in the sun or they would burn to death, but in his mind this was what summertime should smell like.

"I hope I didn't keep you waiting too long," she murmured. The musical lilt to her voice soothed his soul. He could listen to her talk all day.

He swallowed down his desire to jump on her and fuck her into oblivion. It was imperative that he maintain his control. This may be the last female he was ever with and he wanted to savor her as much as possible. "It was worth the wait."

She smiled and it took his breath away. "I thought we could take a swim and unwind. You know, get to know each other. I know we are on borrowed time and need to get to work, but, well honestly, I want to lose myself in your arms and am afraid that if we don't do something about it, I won't be able to concentrate enough to focus on saving you." She smiled again, meeting his gaze and staring deeply into his eyes. The look went straight to his cock and it jerked in response.

He was shocked by her forward nature, but thrilled to hear it. "Then I won't point out that I have no swim trunks with me."

Her laughter was infectious and he was soon joining her. Somehow, her amusement made his dire situation all but disappear. "I only wore the suit for propriety's sake. I normally swim nude. That's why we have so much foliage around the pool." She slipped her feet out of her shoes and glided down the steps into the shallow end of the pool. He was shocked to hear that her sisters didn't mind her flaunting her body around their mates. If she were his, he wouldn't allow another male to see one inch of her luscious body.

He quickly removed his shoes and socks then his shirt and pants. He paused at his briefs, knowing if he went to her naked, he'd be on her in a heartbeat. "I'll keep these on for now. Slow things down." He did nothing to hide the fact that his erection rose above the waistband of his briefs. Truth was, there was no hiding when one was as large as he was.

She lifted her hand and he saw a glint of silver. A ring with a black stone sat on her forefinger. "Bhric," she called and black smoke rose from the ring, encircling above their heads, and turned into a black bat. An actual bat, with wings and everything. "Go feed, sweetie. I'll be busy for a while." Caine recalled stories that had circulated about Bhric, one of the Vampire Princes, being a lover to one of the witch sisters. It was obvious that Suvi was the sister in question. How was he going to compete with that? The other male was a formidable warrior, Caine was a businessman. Not to mention that Bhric was known for his sexual prowess.

"Have you changed your mind?" Suvi asked, tilting her head at him. Seeing the desire in her eyes quickly suffocated his insecurities.

"No, love." He dove into the pool and swam up behind her. He surfaced and pulled her into his arms. She twisted around and looked up at him expectantly.

He tangled one hand in her hair at the nape of her neck while the other wrapped around her waist. He growled low and tugged her flush against him. He lowered his head and pressed his lips to hers. Electricity exploded from every point their skin met. Her lips were soft and inviting and she immediately took charge. She ran her tongue across his lower lip, taking advantage and slipping her tongue into his mouth when his lips parted.

The taste of her exploded across his taste buds and had him wanting to taste every inch of her. His hands roved over her back and followed the indentations at the base of her back then both hands grabbed onto her ass and lifted her against him. He took his time exploring every inch of her mouth while grinding his stiff shaft against her slick core, their clothing adding friction.

"Don't tease me, vampire. If you haven't noticed, I'm a witch and could light you on fire."

"I plan on taking my time tasting every inch of your

body." He held her and walked to the side of the pool. Taking her mouth once more, he reached back and undid her bikini top. She let if fall and float away in the pool. He stood back and gazed at perfection. The beads of water glistened on the rosy tips of her globes. "Goddess, you are beautiful." He grabbed her breasts in both hands and palmed their heavy weight. He dipped his head and licked a bead of water and bit her straining nipple while he squeezed and teased the other. She cried out and arched into him, pushing her flesh further into his hand. She was so damn hot. Zander wasn't going to have to put him to death, he was going to be incinerated right there in the pool.

She clawed at his back then pushed down his briefs, grabbing at his cock. No, he couldn't allow her to touch him or his beast would be unleashed.

SUVI COULDN'T BELIEVE the feel of Caine feasting on her body. She felt a connection with him and it strengthened with each passing moment, adding to the eroticism. As he sucked one nipple into his mouth, sparks of need rippled through her moist feminine flesh. He sank his fangs into the soft tissue of her breast and fed while his hands pulled the ties on her bottoms. The fabric floated away from her and his fingers found her aching core. Her thoughts scattered as he continued to feed and his thick digits slid through her slit and found her throbbing bundles of nerves. She detonated when his finger trailed down, sliding in and out of her pussy.

This was exactly why she preferred vampire lovers. Their bite was orgasmic, but Caine's had her seeing stars. It had never been like this before and she was fiercely glad that she had insisted on bringing him back to their house to discuss their investigation.

"That was just the beginning. Your body knows who its master is," he whispered as he licked the twin pinpricks closed. Yes, her body knew who its new master was, but she wasn't about to let him know that.

"You wish," she croaked as he licked a path down her quivering stomach. His hands reached up to tease her sensitive breasts, and that quick, her need was back with an urgency that was pressing at her. He chuckled as he lifted her easily out of the water and set her on the side of the pool.

His fingers brushed through the black tangle of curls as he continued to kiss her. He had her panting by the time he parted her feminine folds and lowered his head, flicking his tongue from her core to her clit. She felt a flood of cream leave her body with that one touch. "That means nothing," she murmured. He chuckled knowingly against her flesh as he continued his explorations.

He lifted his head and she was caught in the glowing green eyes that echoed her arousal. "See, love, your body knows I am its master and responds sweetly." Keeping his eyes on her, he placed the tip of his rough tongue at her core and inserted it into her. The sensation was devastating. He tongue-fucked her slowly, building her need. She writhed against him, trying to gain more friction where she needed it most. He gripped her hips and held her still, refusing her what she sought.

She saw the wicked glint in his eyes as he drew the tight bundle against the heat of his tongue. He sucked hard and released her hips to insert one of his fingers into her pussy. It wasn't enough, she needed more. The sharp sting at her clit had her holding her breath, hoping he would bite her there. No one had ever done that to her, yet she had yearned to experience it. When his fangs pierced her aroused flesh, she detonated as her thighs gripped his face. Her orgasm came so hard and so fast she wasn't prepared. She was helpless but to writhe in bliss. She swore she left her body.

He must've sensed her body become a boneless mass because his hands caught her and kept her from collapsing, bringing her back down into his arms. As she was lowered back into the heated pool, she wrapped her legs around his waist and felt the hard shaft pressing against her stomach.

She lifted her leg and used her feet to push his briefs off his hips. Strangely enough, she knew this dance with this male. It felt as if they had been doing this forever. It was essential and his body responded just as hers had, with eager enthusiasm. They were both breathless and sweating, their hearts racing, needing more. The way he held himself in check, ramped their arousal even higher.

He brought his lips back to hers and ravaged her mouth. She tasted herself on his lips. Skin on skin, they pressed tightly together, never wanting to separate. She wriggled her body and sighed as his cock slid through her slick channel, rubbing every ultra-sensitive inch. "You are mine, Suvi. I face death and cannot promise you a life together, but I will not let you go until the day I die." She had no idea where his declaration was coming from and all thought left her mind when he tilted his hips back and the mushroomed head was poised at her entrance. He wrapped his hand around her throat possessively, making her a cauldron of liquid fire.

"You will not die, Caine. We will find out who did this," she promised and cried out as he thrust his thick, long shaft into her body in one smooth stroke. He stretched and filled her completely. The feeling of being pushed beyond capacity was a sweet torture. She clung to him, digging her nails into his back as she did.

He pulled back and began to thrust in and out of her slowly while the water added to their overheated skin. His face was beautiful etched with his pleasure. He increased his tempo, each stroke hitting her deeper, harder, fanning the flames of her desire even higher. His name was a ragged plea on her lips, for what, she didn't know.

"I know, love. I know," he whispered and reached between their bodies to pinch her bundle of nerves and she exploded around his cock. She felt like she was floating in the stars and heard him call out her name as he joined her. Sudden, blinding pain had her gasping for a different reason. She scrambled to get away from him, but she couldn't move. She barely registered his identical shout of pain.

She met his confused gaze as his release continued, pouring his hot seed into her womb. And then, she understood what was happening. "Oh, Goddess. It can't be," she whispered. "I'm yours? Your Fated Mate?"

"Yes, love. I had thought this the worst day of my life, but I would go through a million days like this to find you," he professed.

"And, I won't stop until I have saved you. We will have forever, Caine," she vowed, wanting to believe it. She rocked her hips, squeezing his shaft with her inner muscles. His cock jerked, kicking off another set of orgasms for them both.

His shock matched hers as his orgasm continued. His release was like an aphrodisiac, arousing her once more. She may die from the pleasure, but she wasn't going to complain.

"Ah, Goddess, you feel so fucking good." His hips

continued to thrust shallowly and she laid her head on his shoulder. Tears burned her eyes as she neared peak once again. She took the moment into her soul, enjoying the pleasure of their union, unsurpassed as it was, while her heart wept that this may be all they would ever have.

CHAPTER 3

"Pema, Isis," Suvi hollered as she entered the house, Caine right behind her. "Get your asses down here, now!"

She glanced down at her left ankle and the mating brand that still throbbed. It was a crescent moon with a drop of blood at the tip and the whole thing was surrounded by vines. She imagined it would be stunning after they were fully mated. She still couldn't wrap her mind around the fact that Caine was her Fated Mate. Her body was thrumming with the after-effects of their love-making. She had never known pleasure so intense. She hated the fear for his life that was overwhelming everything, destroying what should have been the best night of her life.

"What the hell are you yelling about?" Isis snapped as she walked into the living room.

Suvi stopped in her pacing to glare at her sister. "What's wrong is that we have work to do and no time to waste." She was a loose cannon at the moment and knew she was being unreasonable.

"Oh, but we have time for you to have sex with males

you just met?" Isis countered, her anger spiking, making a lightbulb shatter in a nearby lamp. Caine startled at the noise, looking around in confusion.

"Hey now! Let's settle down before anything else is destroyed," Pema intervened, as she entered the room.

"He's not just some male. He's *my* male. He's my Fated Mate and he has been sentenced to die. We need to get to work finding a way to save him. I can't lose him...I just found him," she declared, sticking her foot out and frantically pointing at the brand on her ankle. She felt strong arms wrap around her and Caine's heat envelop her. She tried to find the comfort he was offering rather than the panic, but it evaded her.

"Oh, Goddess. You've been praying for this since you were a stripling..." Isis trailed off, clearly at a loss for words.

"Okay, calm down. We will figure this out. All of us together, just like we always have. We won't let you lose him," Pema promised. Suvi took several deep breaths, trying to control herself because the last thing they needed at the moment was for Isis to absorb Suvi's emotions and wreck the house.

"Welcome to the family," Ronan told Caine, clapping him on the shoulder.

"It's never a dull moment here, but you'll adjust," Braeden added.

"Is that code for 'these witches are crazy'?" Caine asked with a smile in his voice.

"Hey, we don't hide our crazy around here. We put it in a bikini and prance it around the pool," Isis retorted.

"I know, little flame, and I love it," Braeden told her sister before he kissed her cheek. Suvi appreciated how everyone had immediately welcomed her mate and he fit right in, falling into easy banter with them.

"Speaking of the pool, we need to cancel our birthday party. There is too much going on right now," Suvi added, hating that she had to take the celebration from her sisters, but it was necessary to save her mate.

"When is your birthday? I can't believe you are my mate and I hardly know the first thing about you. We haven't had a chance to talk about anything aside from my...situation," Caine observed. Suvi hated the expression she saw on his gorgeous face.

"Our birthday is in two days. It's been a tradition that we've always had a pool party," Suvi explained, "but we can always have it later, after you're cleared."

"You have a pool party in November?"

"Yes. I'm sure you noticed the spell the sprites cast around our property. It makes the temperature perfect year round," Suvi shrugged, already thinking of the people she'd have to call to cancel. Thankfully the caterer was a fellow witch and a friend and she hoped she hadn't started the cooking yet.

"No, you aren't canceling your birthday party. I don't want to be the reason you cancel anything. The party happens," Caine insisted.

"Not a chance in hell. There is no way I could celebrate right now. My focus is you and finding a way to save your life." Anxiety over the thought of glibly partying while the sand was running out of her mate's hourglass had Suvi's heart racing and her chest constricting.

"You are my other half, Suvi, and your birth should be celebrated. The moment you were born, I was completed, even if I didn't know it before. This party happens," Caine insisted, running a finger down her arm. That one touch alone calmed her, enabling her to breathe. She crossed to the sofas and sat down. Caine sat next to her and the others all followed suit.

"Let's table that discussion for later. Right now, we need to decide where we start," Pema quickly refocused the conversation, kick-starting a plan.

"Based on the information that Caine has provided, I think we go to the scene of the crime. It's the one place we are guaranteed to get answers," Suvi suggested, anxious to be doing something productive.

THE TAINT of evil was still in the air surrounding the house where Sally had died earlier that evening, making Caine's skin itch. His blood and body was still humming from making love to his Fated Mate and now he was forced to return to this location when all he wanted was to be back in bed with Suvi. He hated everything about this situation. He wished that Sally was still alive, but he wouldn't change meeting his mate. He wanted to be celebrating his union with Suvi instead of being worried that he was potentially placing her and her family in more danger.

Putting those considerations aside, he glanced down the quiet street in Madison Park as he approached the dark, single-story home in front of them. The yellow crime-scene tape was still across the front door and the scent of the human authorities lingered, telling him it hadn't been long since they'd left the house.

The scent of Santiago and Orlando mixed with the humans reminded him that it was because of them that he wasn't in a human jail. No member of the Tehrex Realm would do well in a human jail. It would be impossible to hide their supernatural status when surrounded by criminals that would pull at their predatory side. For vampires, it would be a death sentence come sunrise. They had covered up his involvement and he was grateful that they had, but he wondered what the two shifters had thought of the malevolent residue. For Caine, it was like ice in his veins.

His mate's sultry voice warmed his suddenly cold soul and had hers stirring in his chest. "Do we cut through the tape or go around back and break in? Did she give you a key?" Jealousy momentarily glittered in her brown eyes before it was masked. He reached out and tugged on a lock of her black hair.

"No, love, she didn't. Our relationship wasn't like that. I cared for her, but things were not serious. Certainly, not what you shared with Bhric, the *Prince*." He instantly regretted his words when he saw hurt flash across her pretty face and wanted to rewind the moment and take it back. Neither of them came to the relationship innocent and it wasn't fair to judge or bring up the past. Unfortunately, there was no removing the foot from his mouth.

The mating compulsion was bringing out all kinds of emotions. Couple that with the predicament he'd awoken to find himself in and the combination was dizzying. One thing he'd have to keep in mind was that the sense of urgency regarding his life amplified the natural possessiveness and jealousy experienced with a mating. His mate deserved to be treated like a queen, rather than made to feel guilty for what she couldn't change.

He had been through so much in the past few hours and to say he was overwhelmed was the understatement of his three and a half centuries.

"Everyone is on edge. I know what it's like when you are newly mated, but we need to focus on getting evidence of what really happened here. Let's go in through the back," Pema interrupted.

He leaned down and kissed Suvi, pouring all his jumbled emotions into it. He hated to burden her, but she was his mate and carried part of his soul. There was no one better suited to help him through this time in his life. "Your sister is right. My life is in your hands, love, don't hold my blunder against me," he implored. The smile that broke over her face made him weak in the knees.

She stood on her tiptoes and placed a sweet, triumphant kiss on his lips. "I've always held your life in my hands, you just never knew it. Now, let's get this shit done." Suvi grabbed his hand and started walking around to the side fence. He glanced around and saw her two sisters and their mates. Ronan led the group of black-clad trespassers. He was carrying a large duffle bag and it reminded him of Mission Impossible, except for the fact that his mate stalked the night in the sexiest thigh-high boots ever made. He marveled at how she maneuvered so gracefully in the skinny, spiked heels. He'd like to see her in nothing but those boots and a smile before he died.

Pulling his hand from her grasp, Caine placed it at the small of her back, urging her along. He relaxed more when they reached the back yard, out of sight of any neighbors. The last thing he wanted was a nosy neighbor calling the police. The yard was a barren desert compared to Suvi's piece of paradise, adding to the grim atmosphere.

They stepped onto the small, square of concrete that served as Sally's patio and with a flick of their wands, and a one word chant, the witches had the sliding glass door unlocked and opened. The stench of death slapped him in the face as soon as they entered through the kitchen. The house looked the same as it had earlier in the evening, clean and orderly, despite the disgusting odor. They bypassed the small bistro table and chairs, heading straight for the living room.

"Goddess, this reminds me of the smell when I fought those hellhounds," Ronan remarked.

"Ugh, it reminds me of the dark magic Cele was using when she held Donovan captive," Isis added with a curl of her lip. Caine had to hold back his gag when his stomach churned and bile rose to the back of his throat.

It was in the living room that they found evidence that something had occurred in the house. The sofa was askew and the cushions were strewn about the floor. Fingerprint dust littered every surface, thickest on the coffee table. Knowing that supernaturals don't leave fingerprints, he didn't have to worry about the police having any record of him. The chalk outline sent a pang of sadness, reminding him that Sally had lost her life. She didn't deserve the fate that befell her and he wondered what could have possibly led to this incident.

He hadn't told anyone where he was going that night and he didn't really have enemies. He had never been threatened. Hell, he didn't go around getting into fist-fights. The only time in his life that he was in any fights was during his transition to adulthood when all males were volatile due to the influx of hormones and power.

He'd been pondering these issues ever since Zander had asked who might want to set him up or cause problems for him. As far as he knew, Sally didn't have abusive exes or people who wanted to harm her, either. She had no knowledge of supernaturals so how she could have earned the wrath of a vampire was beyond him. Still, he had been wracking his brain for who could have done this and why. Each time he contemplated it, he came up empty-handed.

"Suvi, get the salt and flowers. Isis, light the candles," Pema instructed, catching his attention. "Ronan, help me move this table." The couple picked up the table and maneuvered it into the middle of the room and Isis placed several items on top of it.

"Are you going to be doing this, how do you call it, skyclad, mate?" Ronan asked, waggling his eyebrows suggestively. Caine had heard witches often performed their rituals nude to enhance their power and he wasn't sure how he felt about that. He would never be able to stop Suvi from practicing her craft, and wouldn't want to, but the thought of the other males seeing her naked made him crazy with possessiveness. Suvi belonged to him, no male would ever see her naked again.

"With all these males present?" Pema retorted, arching one of her eyebrows at the bear shifter.

"I have no desire for any other male to see you naked, but I know for a fact that the others will have only eyes for their mates and your nudity will go completely unnoticed. Besides, won't my desire for you boost your magic?" Ronan replied hopefully. Caine knew the truth in Ronan's words, there was no way he would notice anyone but Suvi. And, if he could be more than a burden to his mate, then he was all for it.

Pema laughed at her mate and her expression shifted from business to bliss in a heartbeat. The love the two of them shared was obvious and had Caine yearning for the same. "Not this time, mate. We shouldn't need the extra power for a simple reveal spell because the remnants of the murder are strong here."

Caine watched the witches work silently and efficiently. Suvi drew the circle with salt around the six of them and the sisters cast it and called the elements. He had never seen or felt such strong energy. It raced across his skin, leaving a blazing trail in its path. Suvi clasped his hand and Braeden grabbed his other hand until they had all joined and formed their own circle.

"Live and learn, learn and live. I endeavor to receive what life can give. Bring to me the lessons true. And knowledge of what to do. Amid the mess and chaos fierce. Shine a light to darkness pierce. Show the way to knowledge deep. Which to let go and which to keep. Clear the way so I might heed. The lessons that I truly need. Show me what I need to learn. By the Power of Three, so mote it be," the witches called out in unison.

Mist gathered at their feet and built to surround them. An electrical current raced through his blood. The sensation was erotic and made blood surge to his shaft. He questioned whether or not his arousal had to do with witchcraft or the fact that he was connected to his mate. Embarrassed by his reaction, he tried to drop Braeden's hand, but the magnetic pull binding them refused to let go.

Brilliant, white light emanated from their joined hands and Caine noted that a blue light streamed from between Isis and Braeden's hands and a golden light from between Pema and Ronan's, coloring the area. He looked down at his and Suvi's hands and saw nothing. Clearly, the light was a result of their mating and he felt bereft that he didn't have that with Suvi. Someday, he told himself. He would make it through this ordeal and they would be mated.

He paused in his contemplation, as a sixth sense told him that it was critical to complete the mating ritual with Suvi, sooner, rather than, later. He didn't know why, but didn't think it had to do with the murder he was being accused of. He shook the thought from his mind, concentrating on the matter at hand.

Images formed in the mist and he saw himself sitting with Sally on the couch behind them. They were talking and drinking wine. She threw her head back and laughed at something he'd said and instantly Caine was grateful that he had not so much as touched Sally on that evening as the events played out before them. He didn't think his mate would have handled seeing him with another female very well. He knew that he wouldn't have been able to handle seeing her with another male.

He continued watching and noticed a dark cloud forming behind him in the image. It was disturbing to see it so clearly now, when he hadn't seen anything earlier in the evening. That image slowly solidified into a vampire. He was unforgettable with long, bright-red hair and bi-colored eyes against pale skin. He flashed his fangs in a snarl and threw a small dart into Caine's neck. Caine watched his body slump forward, obviously unconscious.

Sally began screaming as the male stalked her. He backed her up against the wall by her fireplace and picked her up by the throat with one hand. He savagely bit into her neck and drank deeply. Sally fought at first, but that fight slowly dwindled until she was still. The vampire fed several minutes more before tossing her to the ground like a piece of garbage. Sneering, he picked up Caine's slack form and dropped him across the dead human.

He walked to a nearby phone, picked it up and called the police. Before he left, he grabbed the dart from Caine's skin. The vampire seemed completely in control of his actions and Caine wondered how he was able to drain his victim and not be in a blood-induced blackout.

The images faded, the mist dissipated and Isis picked up a knife from the table to open the circle. Suvi turned to him and he saw tears brimming in her eyes. He saw his mate's sadness for Sally's fate, but felt her anger and frustration. "Do you know that male? Why does he hate you so much that he would set you up to die?"

"I have never seen him before. I live a simple life and generally keep to myself. I don't understand why this happened, but this is the break we've needed. This can save me. Let's go show this to Zander, it will prove my innocence."

Suvi's face fell and the tears streamed down her cheeks. Her defeat was clear, but he was confused as to why. "That's not possible. We can't even bring him here and re-cast the spell to show him. Our magic dissolved the memory. It now becomes our word against the evidence. And, despite the fact that he considers us an ally, this won't be enough for him to overturn the sentence. As happy as I am that fate finally brought us together, the sad fact is that now works against us. You are my mate and there isn't *anything* I wouldn't do to save you. And everyone knows my sisters would do anything for me...even lie."

He stared at her as her words sunk in. They'd discovered what had happened and yet he still had no way to prove his innocence. That little sliver of hope vanished, once again leaving him helpless. His heart twisted in his chest and he suddenly couldn't breathe. He refused to be put to an unjustly death. And, especially now that he'd found the missing half of his soul.

Pema placed her hand on Suvi's shoulder. "This isn't the end. We will take this information to Zander and maybe he will know who this male is. He is the king of all vampires. I promise you we will find this vampire and bring him to justice."

It was difficult for Caine to muster any hope that Pema was right as he looked to his watch. The clock was ticking...

CELE WELLS WATCHED as one more scoop of earth was tossed onto an ever growing pile of dirt. The sounds of insects and night creatures joined Marshall's curses. She was furious that Zander and his council had the nerve to bury her daughter, Claire. No doubt those Rowan sisters had insisted that her precious baby be laid to rest so that she was forever beyond Cele's reach.

Cele stifled the urge to hunt them down and end them once and for all. It was their fault Claire was dead in the first place. Only the fact that she needed them alive to relinquish their power to her was saving them at this point. She called her Dark power and watched as a black ball of light formed in her palm. The power rush was immense, but she wanted more. She wanted the power of three. Once she had that, she could rule all of earth, not just the Tehrex Realm.

"Why am I digging up your dead daughter?" Marshall asked, pausing and leaning on the end of the shovel. The night was dark, well past midnight and there was no artificial lighting in the realm cemetery, but her and Marshall could see clearly with their enhanced vision.

She was worried that the wards she'd disabled to get to the gravesite would be detected and quickly scanned the surrounding area to ensure they were still alone. It would not bode well for them to be discovered. "Because, vampire, that demon promised that he would bring Claire back from the dead. That is why you need to get into Zeum and steal that amulet. Surely, as one of Zander's subjects, you can accomplish this." Cele clenched her fists and crushed the black light, reabsorbing the magic. This vampire and his whining were testing her patience.

"It is not as easy as you think. I have no idea where

Zeum is, and even if I did, I have no clue where the Triskele Amulet may be," he groused, still not working. She couldn't take his pathetic demeanor and pulled out her wand, pointing it at the vampire and chanted the ancient spell. Obviously, she needed to reinforce her authority over the male. She couldn't afford for him to break free from her enchantment and gain back his control.

His back arched and his face pulled tight with his pain. After several long minutes she stopped the spell and smiled when he silently returned to his digging. With her plan back on track, she reveled in the fact that soon, all would be within her grasp.

Suvi's mate, Caine, was going to die in less than three days and she would be devastated. She would come to Cele begging to have him brought back to life, willing to give her anything to make that happen. Those sisters of hers would easily agree to Cele's terms to make their sister happy. Knowing how much the sisters loved one another, manipulating them was all too easy.

On the other hand, if Suvi joined with Caine and completed their mating, the triplets would be unbeatable. That was something she would never allow. She recalled feeling the additional power when the sisters had ruined her previous plans and freed that stripling. Her rage over all that had occurred that night sent black sparks shooting from her fingertips. Soon, she vowed, she'd have everything she wanted. Her daughter by her side and ultimate power.

"You had better hurry vampire, before that sun crests the horizon and you burn to a crisp."

CHAPTER 4

Nausea swirled in Suvi's stomach. Her life had been upended in a matter of hours and she no longer knew which way was up. Her body and mind were being torn in different directions. The mating compulsion was driving her crazy with unspent lust while at the same time her stomach was cramped and twisted with fear for the life of her mate. She watched the magic shimmer as they passed through the gates and were admitted to Zeum.

She prayed that Zander would believe them and have information about the red-haired vampire. They needed more evidence for Caine to walk free and she didn't have the slightest idea where to go from here. Warm fingers curled around her hand and squeezed. The knot in her gut unfurled with the contact and she found she was able to breathe easier. The comfort from her Fated Mate soothed her like nothing else. She tried to hide her distress, but ultimately knew it was futile. Their connection that had been growing stronger with each passing second, laid bare their emotions to one another.

Ronan pulled the car under the portico and they were greeted by the majordomo, Angus, a sexy dragon shifter who ran the compound with an iron hand. She marveled at the many layers of protections the Vampire King had woven around him, with Angus being a formidable part. Her eyes widened at the male who stood behind Angus. He was taller than the dragon, but just as muscled and good-looking. His lips curved into a sinful smile that was at odds with the thoughtful expression Angus wore.

Angus approached her door and assisted her out of the car with old world elegance. "Suvi, so good to see you again, lass." She loved his Scottish accent and almost blushed as he brought her hand to his mouth and pressed a kiss to the back of it. At the low ominous growl, she turned her head and smiled at her mate. He was as possessive as her sister's mates were of them. "Good to see you, as well, Caine. I see that you have found your better half." Angus winked at Suvi, his eyes twinkling with humor.

"Thank you, Angus. She is my everything," Caine murmured and twined their fingers together.

"Let me introduce you to one of my people. This is Nate, one of my Máahes. I am training him to take my place here at Zeum. Nate, this is Suvi and her sisters, Isis and Pema and their mates, Braeden and Ronan." Suvi was shocked to hear that Angus was leaving. As far as she knew, Angus had always been with the Vampire King and his household and she wondered how Zeum would fair without him. Somehow, she didn't see Nate filling his shoes.

She would have asked about Angus' departure, but Nate spoke up. "It's a pleasure to meet all of you. I believe I'm going to enjoy it here if visitors to the compound are as beautiful as you three." Suvi recognized a player a mile away and this male was definitely a smooth talker. She glanced at their mates and saw them scowling at Nate and she had to laugh.

"It's nice to meet you, Nate. I've never met another dragon shifter aside from Angus, so I expected your magic to feel like his, but it doesn't," Pema replied. "Is that because you are his Máahes?"

"What is a Máahes anyway?" Isis asked before Pema had finished talking.

Nate chuckled and looked to Angus. "'Tis a long story, but they are my warriors from my home realm of Khoth."

"Your warriors?" Suvi couldn't stop the question from escaping.

"Angus is the King of Cuelebre in Khoth, and as such, he leads us all," Nate answered.

"Wow," Suvi exclaimed, looking at the majordomo. She was shocked to hear that he was the king of dragons and from another realm.

"Nate is correct. I am King of Khoth, but that is a story for another day. I assume the unfortunate situation with Caine is what brings you here."

"Yes, it does," Caine interjected following the change of topic. "Is Zander waiting for us?"

"Aye, he and Bhric are in the war room. Please, follow me." Angus turned and entered the house, the rest of them following closely behind.

"Why did it have to be *that* Prince?" Caine muttered under his breath.

"What?" she asked for clarification, even though she'd heard him clearly. He simply shook his head in response. She knew he was jealous of Bhric, but he had no reason to be. She may have enjoyed numerous trysts with the Vampire Prince, but he didn't hold a candle to her mate.

"Don't be jealous of him. He pales in your light," she

reassured him. She understood all too well how he would feel such an emotion. After all, when she watched the human flirting shamelessly with her mate, she couldn't stop the green monster from rearing its head. It didn't matter that this occurred before they had met one another. The mating made you insane with possessiveness and there was no way to deflect those emotions. Your Fated Mate carried part of your soul and was made for you and no one else, so the thought of that person being with another, past or present, was enraging.

Caine turned and the look he gave her stopped her heart. It held need, desire, love, and so much more she couldn't discern. How could a male show such vulnerability without fear or ego? The Goddess had blessed her with the perfect mate. Surely, she wasn't going to take him from her so soon. She clutched him to her with every ounce of urgency coursing through her. They could not fail to find the culprit and clear Caine's name. She lifted her chin stubbornly as they entered the war room. Come hell or high water, she would convince Zander to help them.

Bhric and Zander were sitting forward in their seats with their arms folded on the large conference table, deep in conversation. They stopped talking and stood the moment they entered the room. Zander was dressed in an Armani suit while Bhric was in his fighting leathers. Suvi noted that the sight of Bhric in his leathers did not affect her like it usually did. It was unbelievable how life could change in such a short amount of time.

Zander looked pointedly at Caine and then their clasped hands. "Please, have a seat. I see you brought the witches. Does this mean you have information for me?"

Caine sat and pulled her into the chair next to him. "There have been many developments since I left your dungeons." Caine's gaze met hers and held for several seconds.

By the time they looked back, Zander had one of his eyebrows imperiously arched. "First, Jace was right about these talented witches being able to help. They were able to perform a spell and replay the night of the murder. We watched as I sat with Sally having some wine and a dark cloud formed before a vampire appeared. He injected me with a toxin that rendered me unconscious immediately. I didn't see him at the time and didn't feel the dart hit my skin." Caine paused when Zander and Bhric's eyes went wide and they looked sharply at each other and then at each of the room's occupants.

"That is no' possible. There isna a toxin that would act so fast in one of us," Bhric uttered in denial.

"Give me all the details you can. And, describe this vampire for me." Zander demanded.

Suvi listened as Caine related everything they had seen in the mist, unable to stop from becoming angry over the entire situation. She appreciated that Zander and Bhric listened attentively and didn't dismiss them outright. She had seen Zander take note of their relationship and worried he may not listen.

"Och, what a bluidy fucking mess. How the hell does one of my vampires transport withoot a portal? And how did he get ahold of this drug? He never should have been awake after drinking the human past death, let alone call the police." Zander paced the room, clearly lost in thought.

"The vampire sounds like Marshall. He is a young male, under two centuries and no' verra powerful. He certainly shouldna be capable of producing such a powerful agent. On the surface, this proves your innocence, but I sense something else is at work here..." Zander pinned them both with his Sapphire-blue eyes. "Can you take me there and show me what you saw?"

Suvi's heart sank at his request. He wanted to believe, like she had hoped, but he needed proof. "No, we can't. The magic we utilized was so powerful it destroyed the memory remnants that clung to the house. And, to put this out on the table, Caine is my Fated Mate. We understand that fact places suspicion on what we are reporting, but it is the truth, nevertheless." Tears burned in her eyes and emotion choked her. She was ready to fall to her knees and beg for her mate's life if that's what it took.

Zander's eyes softened as he watched Caine react to her despair and wrap comforting arms around her shoulders. Bhric broke the tension of the moment. "Damn, another good one gone. Doona worry Suvi. It never would have worked out between us anyway."

Caine lifted his head and glared at the vampire prince, but it was Isis who spoke up. "You're right vamp, because she came to her senses a long time ago."

"Ignore my *brathair*, Caine. He has no idea what tact is and uses humor as a shield. He doesna understand what happens between mates, but I assure you he will work hard to see you cleared. He really does care for your mate," Zander disclosed.

"As long as he understands that she is mine now," Caine growled.

"You mated ones have no sense of humor," Bhric said shaking his head in mock disgust. Suvi didn't buy it for a second, but also knew that Bhric meant well. "Zander is right, Suvi, we won't just sit by and let this happen. We need to find this vampire and get this cleared so you two can live happily ever after," he said and smiled. He was such a smart-ass, one of the things she had found so attractive about him.

"Bhric is right. Find Marshall and bring him to me alive and I will get to the bottom of this. According to his TRex profile, he works as a bartender at Confetti Too. Check with Killian aboot his schedule. Kill will be able to give you an address, too. Most importantly, congratulations on your mating. 'Tis truly a new and exciting time for the realm." Suvi appreciated the confidence Zander offered that she and Caine would make it through this.

Caine leaned forward, intent and determined. "I will find this male, but I get a piece of him after you are done with him. And, I want to mate Suvi, soon. I don't want to wait. Will you perform the ceremony, Liege?"

Suvi saw the startled look in Zander's eyes before he masked it. She guessed the king wasn't used to being asked such things yet. "You will have your piece and I will be more than happy to mate you. I would be honored, actually. But, you are running oot of time."

∾

"Do you see him?" Suvi asked, craning her head around as she scanned the bar again.

"No, dammit. He could be lying low to avoid scrutiny, love. It would be hard to hide the effects draining a human would have on him. It's hard to hide when your eyes are dilated and you are jittery as hell. Anyone here would be able to feel the stain on his soul from such actions," Caine said.

Pema set her drink down and lifted her hand, signaling Killian. "Don't get discouraged, sis. I know this is hard for you both, but trust me, I feel the urgency, as well. I hate that you are both going through this right now. Hey, Kill," she said as the club owner approached their table. "Has Zander spoken with you?"

Killian embraced the witches and shook the males' hands. "It's good to see you all. And, yes, Zander called earlier. Although, I admit I didn't expect to see you tonight with it being so close to sunrise."

Suvi's temper flared. She had always been the easy-going one while Isis was the hot-head, yet she found herself snapping at even the slightest thing. "We have no choice but to be here right now. Caine doesn't have time to wait until tomorrow night, now does he?" she spat and hated the tears that burned her eyes and threatened to spill over. She was not a crier, but along with the temper, had come the tears.

Killian rubbed his hand through his golden hair and his jade eyes reflected his empathy. "I didn't mean to imply that you shouldn't be here or wouldn't be working hard to save him, only that you would be doing what you could while remaining safe from the sun."

Caine smiled and leaned on the table. Caine was a strong, formidable male that shone with light and Suvi admired her mate's composure under pressure. She, however, was about to come out of her skin with anxiety. "What can you tell us about him? When was he here last?"

Killian placed his hands in the pockets of his black slacks and surveyed his club. Suvi had the image of a great lion surveying all he ruled. "He is an easy going male who has never been an issue. The females seem to like him well enough and the males in the club have never had a problem with him. In fact, I've never seen him be aggressive. He has worked almost every night since I hired him, but called in about six days ago and hasn't been seen or heard from since."

He sat down on a barstool at their table. "The last night

he worked I saw him in the parking lot with Cele when I was walking Kim to her car. Zander had already put out word about Cele so it shocked me to see them together. I know it was him because Marshall's hair is hard to miss, you know. I cast a spell making myself invisible then cautiously approached them. As I got closer, I heard her speaking in a foreign tongue that I didn't recognize. It was a harsh and rough language and as soon as she was done speaking, Marshall's demeanor changed. Cele must have sensed my presence and she barked at him to get in her car, but there was no mistaking that it was as if he was a puppet waiting for its master. I tried to follow them..." Killian lowered his head and shook it sadly.

"You have got to be fucking kidding me! We should have known that bitch was involved. You were right, Isis, the oily feel of death in that home was Cele. Shit!" Suvi exclaimed. They needed to find that unholy no-good excuse for a witch and take her out of everyone's misery. In fact, she couldn't begin to count the number of ways she wanted to rip Cele limb from limb.

"Why the hell would she target Caine? And, why set him up to be executed?" Pema postulated.

Isis' eyes widened and she leaned over the table, slapping her palms on the tabletop. "She's targeting your mate, like she did mine. That is the only way that she can weaken us or have a hope of gaining our power." Her sister's eyes darkened with her fury and the lightbulbs began to break around them. "She will not succeed."

Some of the nearby patrons began looking around at what was causing the destruction. "Isis, calm down. The club hasn't been open that long and I don't want to run patrons off. They are still skittish after what happened last time," Killian whispered

"But why kill him? She should want them together. He will give her more power," Isis continued without acknowledging Killian, but Suvi noticed she was calmer. "Surely, you felt the increase in mine and Pema's power? Hell, you're not even fully mated and I felt the spike in yours. I don't understand it, but I think Cele has targeted him because he is yours."

Suvi's mind was reeling. It was impossible to believe that Cele had found a way to determine their mates, but she obviously had. Caine wrapped his arm around her waist and changed the subject. "I don't have much time, Killian. Do you know where he lives?"

Killian grabbed a napkin and pulled out a pen, writing down the address then handed it to Caine. "I'm sorry I didn't report Cele's suspicious behavior sooner. Honestly, it slipped my mind. Let me know what else I can do to help. Sunrise is upon us, I hope your car has tinted windows. Good luck."

CHAPTER 5

T he sun was cresting the horizon, turning the sky pink and orange. Caine had never before seen the sun and just the lightening of the grey sky was burning his retinas. "Here, put these on," Suvi ordered as she handed him some dark sunglasses. "I can feel the pain in your eyes and these will help. I'm going to call in some reinforcements to meet us at the house."

Caine wanted to laugh at his mate's high-handed behavior, but he found a strong female enticing. Aside from his parents, no one had ever taken care of him, and it touched him to have his Fated Mate with him in his greatest time of need. He pulled on the leather jacket he had borrowed from Braeden and flipped up the collar. His heart began racing in his chest as the sun rose higher. He felt the pain through the layers of clothing and slunk down in the seat below the window. He shouldn't be out here during the day, it was too much of a risk, but he had no choice. He was quickly running out of time.

Every vampire was taught from birth that the sun's UV rays were lethal. He never forgot the lesson his mother taught him at three years old when he wanted to go out and play in the snow. Out of exasperation from his begging, his mother took his hand and held it in a thin shaft of sunlight. His skin turned red and bubbled up immediately. He screamed from the pain and she quickly jerked it back, placing a healing cream on the burn, all the while lecturing him.

Suvi's melodic voice reached through the haze of pain and memories. The UV rays were relentless and he wondered how long he would last under these circumstances. "Santiago, its Suvi. I don't know if you've spoken with Zander or been updated on the situation, but, in short, Caine is my mate, we discovered who set him up, and are headed to Marshall's house right now to try and find him." He closed his swelling eyes and focused on her melon scent which helped his discomfort.

"Yeah, I know its daytime, but we can't wait. Are you and Orlando working today? We need you to meet us and create a storm with thick cloud cover." He had no idea Santiago had the power to manipulate the weather.

A particularly bright stream of light shone through the window and Caine grimaced in silence. He wanted to shield as much as he could from Suvi, not wanting to worry her more. He shut his eyes tighter, but the burning was so intense that he couldn't stop the tears that were now streaming from his eyes. He lifted his hand to shield his eyes and felt blisters forming. Soft fabric settled over his head and clenched hands, dimming some of the effect. He turned his face into the back of the seat, but it wasn't enough. They needed to get to the house and get inside, now.

"Okay, great. We will meet you there in five minutes. And, thanks so much. I owe you one," Suvi said, ending her call.

"Okay, babe, Santiago is going to meet us and create some cloud cover. He and Orlando aren't far from us. In fact, he was going to try and send a storm ahead of them. Just hold on." Suvi rubbed his arm trying to comfort him, but at that point, even that was not enough to alleviate the pain. As Suvi crooned to him softly about how they were going to find evidence and clear his name and then get mated, he felt the strength of the sun lessen and knew the Dark Warrior had delivered on his promise.

Before long, they were stopping and the sky was full of thick grey clouds. It didn't take away all of the effects of the sun, but it was enough of a relief that Caine was able to crack his eyes open a slit. They were in the back of a large SUV and Suvi's sisters and their mates were in the seats in front of them. Ronan turned from the driver's seat and met his eyes. "You look like shit, buddy. Don't worry about anything but bolting for the door once we stop."

Pema interrupted her mate. "I hate to say this, but we aren't going anywhere yet. I can feel the protections that are in place. They are weak and can easily be dismantled, but we can't approach before they are taken care of."

Just his fucking luck. He was close to shelter and one more roadblock was preventing him from reaching it. He would curse fate to hell and back if it weren't for Suvi. Caine heard soft chanting and saw white light fill the car. The warm tingle of magic hurt his burned skin. The pain was overwhelming and he thought he may throw up or pass out, but wasn't sure which would come first.

The next thing he knew, he was being dragged out of the car and up the front walk by Suvi and Ronan. He couldn't remember a time when he had felt so weak or in so much pain. When the door slammed behind him, he heard yelling and screaming while his naturally rapid healing took over and began to repair damaged skin. At the same time, a horrid stench in the house slammed into him.

"I should have known we'd find you here given that you have nothing and nowhere else to go. You aren't going to win this one, Cele. My mate isn't going to die and you will never have our power," Suvi promised.

An evil, raspy voice screeched. "That is where you are wrong. I will have your power. The only way to save your mate's life is to give me what I want." Caine felt the Dark compulsion reaching out to encompass him and knew it was pressing on the others as well. His strength had returned with the absence of the sun beating down on him and his eyes were healed enough to fully open.

He took in the scene around him, and if he hadn't known his eyes were completely healed he'd have thought he was seeing things. The High Priestess stood next to the red-haired vampire, Marshall. Suvi had described Cele as a librarian type, but the female before him had on dirty and disheveled clothing, her hair was falling out of its bun and she had a wild look in her eyes. Marshall looked the same as he had in the vision.

What was shocking and captivated Caine's attention was the dead female lying on the coffee table. Her skin was grey and rotting. His stomach lurched at the sight of the maggots wriggling in and out of her flesh. That certainly explained the foul odor. Given the way the High Priestess clung to the dead female, he assumed this must be her daughter, Claire.

"You are too weak to overpower us now, Cele. We have found our mates and the power of three is magnified. Bet you didn't think we'd figure that out all on our own," Pema taunted. "That's right, we know why you have worked so hard to have Suvi's mate eliminated. We are more powerful with them at our sides. Do you feel that guilty for killing your daughter that you went and dug her up? You really are sick." Pema pointed to the dead female on the table, confirming Caine's suspicions.

"I didn't kill her! That was you three, with your magic! And, you will pay for that with your mates and your power!" Caine could easily see that Cele was driven by fanaticism. A person so blindly driven by obsessive enthusiasm was a frightening force, and with Cele, it was made worse by the dark power behind her zeal.

Isis stepped forward with her hands clenched at her sides, light crackling in them. The lights began to flicker and he recalled what Suvi had told him about Isis being a hot-head and absorbing the emotions of others. This had the potential to be explosive. Suvi and her sisters could be frightening and he was glad they were on his side. "It was not our magic. You have gone Dark and your attempt to have a demon possess Claire's body killed her. You kidnapped and tortured an innocent stripling. You cut him and were going to kill him. You are the monster!" Isis lunged forward and Braeden grabbed her arms, holding her back.

Thunder and lightning roared outside the house. He looked out the window and saw bolts of light striking the ground around an imposing male. He recognized the bald, shifter from his visit to Zeum. Santiago raised his arms, calling the power of the storm to him.

"I merely had the courage to grasp a power that most fear. It is this power and its master that will bring my precious Claire back." Cele flared her fingers and black light danced between them.

The three sisters were moving toward each other when the first blast hit the wall beside Caine's head. Cele had thrown a ball toward his head while he was distracted. Obviously, this bitch really wanted him dead. He had no way of defending himself against a magical attack. He wanted to pull Suvi behind him when she stepped in the line of fire. She nodded to her sisters and they began lobbing white balls of magic at Cele.

"Stay behind me," Suvi instructed. Having her defend him went against his every instinct. He was supposed to protect his mate, yet he knew he had no choice. He was awed at her courage and skill when she didn't hesitate to join her sisters in the fight. He noticed that Ronan and Braeden stayed close to their mates, maintaining physical contact, but not interfering and he did the same.

Pema took a hit in the shoulder and her mate roared his anger, shaking the walls. Santiago answered the call with an increase in the storm. Wind whipped through the trees, thunder rolled and rain slammed into the house, covering the noise of the fight. Isis and Suvi worked in unison to counter the attack. They missed Cele and brick and mortar went flying from the fireplace as the spell hit it instead. Pema lifted her hand to Isis and she grabbed both Pema and Suvi at the same time.

"Marshall! Grab Claire," Cele yelled. Caine watched as the vampire bent and picked up the dead female. The writhing, wriggling, mass of bugs left behind on the table was a disgusting sight. It must be a strong enchantment that the vampire was under given that he followed orders without question and held the rotting corpse close to his body. For a moment, Caine actually felt bad for Marshall and his lack of free will in this matter. There was no doubting that Cele was using him as her puppet.

"Oh, no, you don't," Suvi yelled and threw light at the pair. This time it hit an invisible wall and bounced back. Caine was even more awed as he watched Suvi step in front of the light as it rebounded and absorb it back into her body.

"I need all the power I can get right now and it was mine to begin with," she answered his unspoken question. "Although, I can feel the taint from its brush against her shield. It's like I have a film of oil in my veins," she finished, grabbing his hand and tugging him with her as she stepped back to her sisters.

"That's not going to work this time," Cele spat as she lobbed black fire in their general direction. It wasn't aimed anywhere in particular, but it forced them to separate. Suvi and her sisters threw spells at Cele and she retaliated each time. The pattern repeated over and over again until the room around them was destroyed. Shards of glass, pieces of wood and white stuffing littered the ground.

Caine noticed that Cele was unable to lower her shield long enough to actually hit one of them, but that wasn't really her purpose, he realized. She was keeping them apart and had managed to drive them across the room from one another. He recalled how they had all joined hands at Sally's house and knew that she was stopping them from accessing their combined power.

Caine may not be able to defend against the magic, but he could help his mate reach her sisters. He pulled Suvi into his side and dove for the other side of the room. He ignored the burning pain in his side that told him he had been hit and stood up, bringing Suvi with him. Somehow, Pema and Ronan had reached Isis and Braeden at the same time they did.

Suvi reached for Isis and the moment all six of them were connected, he felt the same surge of magic he'd felt when they cast the spell at Sally's house. Erotic electricity raced through him and he had a moment to panic thinking that he'd have the same reaction as before. An erection was the last thing he wanted right now, but there it was, and in the end, didn't matter one bit. It was, he realized, a side effect of connecting to his Fated Mate and he easily focused on the bigger issue at hand, which was Cele.

The panic was clear in the High Priestess' eyes as she began chanting rapidly and waving her hands in the air. Thick, black smoke grew on the other side of the barrier. He felt Suvi and her sisters throw a spell at the High Priestess and he expected it to rebound back to them, but it didn't. Black fire leapt in Cele's eyes as she spat, "You peasants will not win this. I have power such as you cannot even begin to fathom behind me."

The storm continued to rage outside. The High Priestess reached for Marshall and her dead daughter, but jerked her hand back. Caine noticed her palm was smoking and she had to pat out the flames. She uttered several more spells to no avail. She wasn't able to reach Marshall and looked like she was ready to explode from frustration while the vampire stood motionless with his burden. Cele cast one last, longing look at her dead daughter then screeched before she finally gave up and disappeared in the black smoke.

Caine wondered what Suvi and her sisters had done to prevent Cele from reaching Marshall, but foremost in his mind at the moment was they had the vampire and the proof he needed. They had to get him and the body to Zander. Question was... where were they going to put the decayed female?

As if reading his mind, Suvi blurted, "I don't care what we do, but Veggie-Tales isn't going in the back seat with me. You can strap her to the fucking roof and we can cast an invisibility spell on her nasty ass."

CHAPTER 6

C aine jumped out of the car as soon as they were under the cover of the portico at Zeum. Angus was there to lower the UV shades to block out all sunlight. "Fuck, that is so damn disgusting," he cursed, brushing maggots off the sleeves of the leather jacket and jeans and Suvi couldn't help but laugh at the comical sight of a grown male hopping around. Her laughter died as she was mesmerized by the way his muscular arms rippled while he frantically rid himself of the bugs. He was the sexiest male she had ever laid eyes on and she thanked the Goddess for making him for her.

"Stop it, you big baby. I was back there with you, it wasn't that bad," she teased.

"You could have included me in that little repellant spell you cast. I will make you pay for that mate," he growled as his swollen eyes began to glow with his arousal, obviously aware of her response to him.

She wound her arms around his neck and ran her hands up and down his back. "But then what excuse would I have to get this close to you? Besides, I did it to distract you from the pain of the sun. You were so worried about our extra-smelly cargo that you didn't give the UV rays one more thought." She stood on her tiptoes and brought her lips to his. They were cracked and peeling and what started as a gentle kiss quickly deepened and threatened to go completely out of control. With the sun having finally set, his natural healing abilities kicked in and she soon felt smooth, firm lips.

One of his fangs sliced her lower lip, and he sucked it into his mouth, feeding briefly. The sensation was like nothing she had ever experienced and she melted into his body. The world around them disappeared, and that fast, she was primed and aching to make love to her mate.

"Alright, you two, enough of that. This matter is not yet resolved, you know. Let's go inside and get this over with. As soon as we clear Caine's name, you can go at it all you want," Isis called out over her shoulder as Braeden pulled a restrained and silent Marshall from the car. Suvi reluctantly broke away from Caine's mouth and noted that Marshall fared much worse than Caine during the car ride. The skin on his face and hands had blistered and peeled away, leaving raw flesh exposed. His eyes had likely been swollen shut at one point, but his lids had burnt away and his eyeballs were a gooey mess. There were patches of his red hair missing and his ears hung nearly to his shoulders. It was a vile sight.

"What the hell are we doing with this one? Somehow I doubt that Zander will want us to cart that corpse through the house," Caine observed.

"Nay, we doona want that in the house. I have procured a special freezer that is located in the garage until Zander decides what is to be done with her," Angus said. "Zander and the others are waiting for you inside. Nate will show you the way."

"Why do I have to show them the way? Don't they already know it? They were here just a few hours ago," Nate protested.

Angus turned on him and glared at the other dragon. "As I've told you before, as majordomo, your job is to escort visitors into the house and see to their needs."

"I can't believe our King has been a servant all this time," Nate replied and began walking into the house not bothering to invite them to follow him. Suvi smiled and grabbed Caine's hand. Yep, Nate definitely had his work cut out for him. One thing was certain. Zeum wouldn't be the same without Angus.

Zander and his mate, Elsie, were standing in the door to the war room waiting for them. Pema had called him and informed him that they had found Marshal and were heading back with him, as well as, Claire's body.

"Kyran," the Vampire King called out in his thick Scottish brogue. "Take the vampire doon to the dungeon and give him blood. He needs to heal before we question him. Everyone else, please come in." He gestured to the room behind him.

She grabbed her mate's hand and they found a seat at the same table they had sat at only hours before. Nerves suddenly attacked her like a million writhing snakes in her stomach. Her heart sped up and she told herself to breathe. They had the male responsible and her mate was not going to be put to death, but she wasn't going to be able to relax until she heard the king declare that Caine was cleared. Even then, she wouldn't stop worrying. She knew Cele and had no doubt that she was going to retaliate. Desperate people did desperate things and that female was beyond help.

"I see you found Marshall. I tried to access his mind when he was brought in but I wasna able to. I came up against a bluidy block. After he heals from the ravages of the sun, I will try again. I have to say, I've always been able to read one of my subjects, so whatever Cele did, it was verra potent. Shite, will someone please fill me in on what happened?" Zander asked with his fingers steepled under his chin. He sat back in his chair looking imperial.

"We went to Marshall's house and found Cele there, too. Suvi and her sisters fought with the High Priestess and stopped her from escaping with Marshall and Claire," Caine replied, keeping his response short and sweet.

"Cele was in the middle of writing Dark runes in blood around her daughter when we got there," Pema added. "And, Marshall was completely under her thrall. He stood there like a zombie until she gave him an order. I've never seen anything like it."

"What was she doing?" Elsie asked, joining the conversation.

Pema sat back and folded her arms across her chest. "I believe she was attempting to preserve Claire's body. She mentioned having been given great power and was convinced she could bring Claire back."

"Did she admit her culpability?" Zander asked, getting right to the point.

"Not exactly. She said that I was going to die and it would force my mate and her sisters into relinquishing their power in exchange for bringing me back to life."

"How the hell does she plan on doing that? Last time I checked, it was impossible to raise the dead," Zander demanded, glancing at Suvi and her sisters. "Is this all part of the dark magic she has sold her soul to? Och, the thought is ludicrous."

"You have no idea. She has plans to raise Claire and she is little more than rotting flesh," Isis added. "Can you imagine her walking around with bugs and missing flesh?"

"I don't care about Cele or Claire. We can discuss all that later. What I want right now is for you to exonerate Caine," Suvi snapped, anxious to have her mate safe.

"Suvi," Pema reprimanded.

"No, Pema. Don't Suvi me. I need to know he is safe. I can hardly breathe," she panted as her heart raced in her chest.

"Suvi," Zander captured her attention. "I willna pass judgment one way or another just yet, but I will tell you that the death sentence that was to be executed tomorrow has been stayed until my investigation is complete. I have to question Marshall and that canna happen in his current condition."

Caine wrapped his arm around her waist and pulled her chair close to him. She wanted to crawl into his lap and burrow into his chest. She calmed at the contact, not realizing how much she needed him. She was beyond ready for this nightmare to end.

"How long will it take for him to come around?" Suvi asked.

"I have no idea. The problem is that we doona know who she is working with and what power she used," Zander answered as he ran his hands through his shoulder-length black hair. Of course, Suvi cursed their luck. It seemed they made one step forward but took two back every step of the way. Rather than feeling closer to the finish line, they were back at the start.

Caine took off the leather jacket he had been wearing

and laid it across the back of the chair. He jumped when a lone maggot fell off his bare arm. Suvi's laugh escaped her as a giggle and she smiled at his scowl. "I need a shower. Those damn things are everywhere." He shook his head and addressed his king. "Cele didn't say who she was working with, but vaguely referred to a forbidden power and its master."

Elsie looked up at Zander and they shared a private look. "She willna succeed in either of her goals. We need to know who she is working with. There is a new archdemon and he is far more lethal and cunning than those that came before him. 'Tis possible he has a hand in this. Although, what he hoped to gain from it is a mystery." Zander got up and crossed to an intercom.

"Kyran. Has the vampire been given blood?"

"Aye, he has."

"Has he come around yet?"

"Nay, he hasna said a word yet."

"Bring him to me," Zander ordered and released the button before turning back to the room.

"You said there was a block in his mind. What kind of a block? We may be able to help with that," Suvi interjected. They may not have attended Cele's academy and received the formal education about witchcraft, but there was no power greater than the power of three.

"I canna say for certain what it was and I'm no' certain that it can be dismantled with a spell. You're the experts in this area. Do you think you can break it withoot causing brain damage?" Zander asked, leaning against the wall.

Pema and Isis tilted their heads and met her gaze, more than likely thinking the same thing Suvi was. It was a huge risk. White or light magic's purpose when encountering dark magic was to obliterate it. That didn't bode well for keeping the mind intact. "I can't safely say that we wouldn't cause permanent damage. I won't risk Suvi's mate for expediency, especially, when we have been granted a stay of execution. The stakes are too high," Pema answered, glancing at her and Suvi felt the tears brim in her eyes.

She loved her sisters, and they had a connection almost as strong as the one she was developing with Caine. They understood if Caine didn't live, neither would she. You can't live without your other half. "We are going to have to trust that you will be able to get the information you need from him."

Isis leaned forward in her chair restlessly. "And, you won't be doing anything without a promise that if you fuck up, Caine lives." Suvi heard the determination in her sister's voice.

Zander smiled at the three of them. "You three are a formidable bunch. I wouldna dream of failing." Kyran walked in at that moment guiding Marshall. Behind them, a human female followed closely. Suvi briefly wondered who the beautiful female was. She had an arm full of tattoos and short, spiky black hair and was wearing a t-shirt that said 'I Love My Bloodsucker.' Suvi raised an eyebrow and shared a look with her sisters. Her unspoken question was answered a minute later when she went to stand next to Kyran, who smiled at her and wrapped his arm around her waist. This must be the Prince's Fated Mate.

The room had fallen silent at their entry and Zander pulled out a chair at the table in front of him. "Put him in this chair, *brathair,*" Zander ordered. The vampire allowed himself to be guided freely, giving no fight in the matter. He didn't even look around the room. She prayed to the Goddess that Zander was able to get the answers they needed.

Zander stopped behind the male. "Marshall, 'tis your king. Can you hear me?"

The male turned his head stiffly and met the king's Sapphire blue eyes. There was no recognition in them, but something snapped to attention. "Am I at Zeum?" the vampire asked in a monotonous tone.

Kyran and Zander shared a look before Zander responded. "Aye, lad. You are. Can you tell me what Cele has instructed you to do?"

Marshall's head remained tilted at an odd angle that seemed like it would be uncomfortable, and his voice held no inflection. "I must get the Triskele Amulet," he muttered.

"What the fuck?" Kyran snapped, pivoting to block the doorway. Suvi saw that Kyran's mate pulled a knife from the back of her pants and was standing at the ready next to him. Marshall ignored the outburst and kept repeating that he must find the amulet. At one point, he tried to stand up and walk away, but the king and his brother held him in his seat.

"Let's go in together, *brathair,*" Zander instructed Kyran. Both males closed their eyes while they held the vampire to his chair. For several long, excruciating minutes Marshall kept up his monologue while they scanned his mind.

Suvi cried out when Marshall began convulsing violently. She reached out for her sisters' hands, trying to think of a spell they could cast while Caine and Ronan jumped up to help hold the vampire. Zander and Kyran never once opened their eyes and their concentration didn't waver. After several excruciating minutes, the king and his brother opened their eyes. At the same moment, Marshall slumped in his chair. His head fell to the side and a trickle of blood leaked out of one ear and slowly made its way down his neck.

Suvi's hands flew to her mouth. "Is he dead? No. No, no,

no...he can't be! He has to admit what he did and clear Caine!" she screamed out her denial.

"He is dead, lass. Doona worry though, we were able to retrieve the information we needed," Zander replied, quickly releasing the dead vampire's shoulder. "'Tis unfortunate that this male was used and killed by such evil. Cele targeted him because she needed a vampire and he was easily controlled. He was under her compulsion from the beginning. I saw her order him to kill the human and set up your mate, Suvi. I also witnessed the scene you described earlier. Caine, you are officially cleared of all charges. There will be no execution. However, you all face far more danger than you can fathom. Cele is working with the archdemon, Kadir, as well as another dark being. She mentioned another partner, but didn't give a name."

Suvi was overwhelmed with relief and little of what Zander said after that registered. Nothing else mattered once she heard that Caine was going to live. For the first time since she had met her mate, she fully relaxed. They weren't out of danger yet, but that didn't stop the unadulterated joy that exploded through her as she realized they were going to be mated. But, first things first. Their birthday party, and for her, a new pair of shoes, the higher the better.

CHAPTER 7

"Where do you want this?" Suvi turned at the sound of a familiar voice. The blonde witch had her hands full with a platter of finger sandwiches.

"Courtney, thank the Goddess you're here. Give me a minute and I'll get the food table in place," Suvi replied. She'd been running around like crazy and was glad to see it all coming together. She glanced at the sky and saw that the sun hadn't quite set. She had never been more anxious for nighttime to arrive. She hadn't given the bright orb a second thought until she met her vampire mate who could die by that light.

"No problem. Do you need help with that?"

"Nah, I've got it," she replied, pointing her wand at a stack of folding tables next to the deck. "A *bhogadh*." The moment the spell left her lips, two of the tables lifted into the air and sailed overhead to her side. She waved her hand and they landed at her feet.

"That is so cool, Aunt Suvi. I love watching you do

magic. Dad was right. All magic isn't evil," Donovan muttered as he walked over and stood next to her.

The young male had been playing with one of the sprites nearby and came closer when she cast the spell. They had been careful not to perform magic around him since his ordeal. Everyone had been concerned that seeing it would cause him trauma. She masked the rage that always surfaced when she thought about the horrendous torture he had been through at the hands of Cele.

She turned to him and ruffled his brown curls. "In our world, magic is life and light and it's a very good thing. Now, run and grab me those silver tablecloths from the kitchen."

"Okay," he called out as he took off running.

She looked over and noticed that Isis had been watching them. Her sister gave her a smile and continued decorating. Suvi unfolded the tables and set them up while she contemplated how much the addition of a stripling had changed the way they celebrated. Before, their parties revolved around general debauchery, and she had no doubt that there would be plenty of that tonight, but that would occur behind closed doors. There was a different focus for her and her sisters now.

"You can put the food down here," she instructed Courtney.

"He's an adorable stripling and clearly loves his Auntie," Courtney observed after she had placed her burden down.

"Yes he is and don't tell Pema, but I'm his favorite. It was all those hours playing XBox with him," she laughed.

"That'll do it. I'll be back with the rest." Courtney turned and headed back to her van for the rest of the food and Suvi continued with her task.

She was setting up chairs when Donovan came running. "Here you go," he said handing her the silver fabric. "Can you inflate these now? I want to show them to Fen. She's never seen one," he explained, bouncing up and down with excitement, thrusting a bag of balloons into her hand. Donovan's intrusion caused several chairs to crash to the cement and fall into the pool.

"Oops," he laughed. His laugh was carefree and infectious and Suvi was helpless but to laugh with him.

Still laughing, Suvi looked over at the sprite who was wearing pale-pink marshmallow flowers strung together to make an exquisite dress that offset her fiery-orange butterfly wings for the party. Fen had been one of the first sprites to join their garden. When she had crashed into their lavender bush, she had immediately lit a fire in Suvi's heart. The poor female had been attacked by an Unseelie creature she had called a soul-sucker. Suvi and her sisters had offered her sanctuary and she'd been there ever since. She and Donovan had gone through similar experiences and it wasn't surprising that they had become fast friends.

Fen used to live in reed marshes and lonely fenland and had re-created that in a hidden corner of their property that she'd claimed as her own. Fen could only be seen when the first leaves fell from the trees unless she decided to reveal herself. It was a testament to her affection for them that she was showing herself this night when the confirmed guest list had topped one hundred a few hours ago.

"I will blow them up after you help me put these tablecloths on the tables so that Courtney can do her thing with the food," Suvi offered.

"Awesome, c'mon." He grabbed Suvi's hand and dragged her back to the tables.

"Take this end," she told Donovan as she handed him two corners of the silver fabric and they quickly covered both tables.

"Okay, now blow them up. C'mon Fen, come closer," Donovan called out to his tiny friend. The excitement danced in his blue eyes as she opened the bag and pulled out a red latex balloon. The sprite landed on his shoulder and watched her with equal enthusiasm.

"*Seid*," she chanted and the red balloon inflated and floated next to her head. Donovan was jumping up and down and snatched the balloon, waving it at the sprite. "Careful or you'll pop it. If that happens so close to Fen it'd be really loud for her sensitive ears. Suvi inflated several more balloons and muttered an impervious spell so they could play with them freely. Laughing at their antics, she continued to fill each and every balloon until she was completely surrounded by the colorful decorations.

All of the balloons were inflated within minutes and were seemingly everywhere. This wasn't going to work. They'd never had so many at previous parties so she had to stand back and scope the area. An idea came to her and she cast a barrier five feet above the tree-line and sent the balloons to hover just beneath it. Satisfied, she turned back to find Caine standing behind her.

"Oh, when did you get out here?"

"A few minutes ago. You are stunning when you do magic. And, I can see that you thrive on celebrations," he replied, pulling her into his arms.

He lowered his head to hers and kissed her tenderly. She melted against his body and wrapped her arms around his neck. Just as things were about to get interesting, a throat clearing nearby broke them apart. She looked over her shoulder at Isis.

"Caine can help finish setting up the tables, but you need to get ready now or you will miss the party. People will be arriving in less than an hour. Besides, I have to show you what Braeden gave me," Isis said, pulling her along behind her.

Caine shrugged his shoulders, smiling at her retreating form. "See you soon, love."

She blew him kisses before she disappeared through their back door. Once inside the house, Isis let go of her hand and they walked side by side. "What did he get that has you so eager to show me?" Suvi asked, caught up in her sister's giddiness. Love really did make people act differently. Isis wasn't normally so happy-go-lucky and it made Suvi's heart sing. She still wouldn't want to piss Isis off, her temper was still below the surface...the surface just looked different.

"He made me this," Isis said, doing her best Vanna White imitation, show-casing what was hanging on the wall above her bed. Suvi gasped as she quickly entered the room and crossed to the metal sculpture. It was two, large, silver, intertwining hearts. They weren't perfect hearts by any means, but more abstract in nature and beautiful because of it.

"That is gorgeous. I love it. Your mate is extremely talented. I should ask him to make a mushroom sculpture for the sprites in the backyard, one big enough for Donovan to play on too."

"He is the best," Isis preened. "You can talk to him about it later. Go get ready." She pushed her in the direction of her room and turned back down the stairs.

"You aren't actually wearing those shoes tonight are you?" she called over her shoulder. They were three-inch, red heels that had no sparkle or design. Shoes, in Suvi's opinion, should be at least six inches high and include at least two different fabrics or leathers, straps and bling.

"Sure am," Isis retorted before closing her bedroom

door.

Suvi shook her head and entered her bedroom, crossing to her closet, glad that she had planned her outfit ahead of time. She couldn't show up downstairs without the perfect shoes. The plastic bin sat on her top shelf, waiting to be opened. She picked it up and lifted the lid. What was it about a new pair of shoes? Her sisters thought her crazy, but for Suvi they were exhilarating.

The right shoes could make you look like a million bucks while the wrong ones could have the Fashion Police showcasing you on TRex, the social media network for the Tehrex Realm. She shuddered at the thought and hoped that Isis didn't end up on the cover next week.

She held one eight-inch stiletto to the light. The snake skin and black patent leather straps had drawn her to the shoes, but it was the hot-pink platform at the ball of the foot that really set them apart. She grabbed her black mini dress and went back into her room. She quickly stripped down and slipped on the sexy, little number. It was simple in the front with spaghetti straps and a deep V at the bust. The crisscrossing straps that made up the back of the dress showed off her pale skin.

Smoothing the fabric into place, she contemplated her hair. Finally, she settled on pulling her hair into a high ponytail. She lined her brown eyes in coal and added shimmery eyeshadow. A quick application of lip gloss and she was donning her shoes. She stood up and crossed to her full-length mirror and admired her image.

She turned her ankle, glancing at her mate mark. The crescent moon tipped in blood had been burning since they'd had sex and that pain had only worsened, but, the shoes made the brand look incredible, she surmised. She didn't understand why people would complain about wearing heels. For her, they were the most natural thing in the world. She took one last look in the mirror and realized she was missing something. The final touch to any outfit was always the earrings. She put on her favorite large silver hoop earrings and headed out the door.

The noise from the party increased as she descended the stairs. Butterflies fluttered in her stomach. This was the first party she'd attend with her mate. She was no longer a single witch, ready to prowl the night. A smile spread across her face as she thought about how she was so much better...she was mated.

She stopped at the back door and glanced around, grateful that her sisters had added the finishing touches. Isis had dragged her away before she'd cast the lights, but they had done it for her. Multi-colored orbs floated amongst the balloons giving the area its illumination. It was too much color in her opinion and she muttered a spell to switch all the lights to clear. She observed her work and nodded. Much better, now only the balloons provided the color.

She strode out and her eyes immediately sought out Caine. She was glad to see the Dark Warriors in attendance as she noticed Santiago and Orlando by the food table talking to a couple of Valkyries. They were brave males. Valkyries were lethal assassins. Gerrick was scowling at the pair a few feet away, obviously not happy to be there. He wasn't one to wear a smile on his face, but he wasn't typically pissed off and she wondered what was going on with him. Jace and Cailyn were tossing a ball to Donovan who was in the water and Zander and Elsie were nearby watching the interaction. Unless she was mistaken, those were looks of yearning in Elsie's eyes. Suvi smiled at the thought of babies taking over Zeum.

She quickly scanned through dozens of other people

and found Caine standing next to Nate, deep in conversation. She noticed that Caine had changed into black dress pants and a green silk button down that matched his eyes perfectly. His lean muscled body and the way his head swiveled to follow her movements caught her breath and once again reminded her of a black panther. His glowing gaze held an intensity that spoke of his predatory nature. She shuddered as she recalled the feel of his fangs sinking into her breast. Her nipples hardened at the thought and she flushed with arousal. A magnetic pull had her sauntering in his direction. There were no words spoken between them but she knew what he wanted. She wanted it too, right now, if she had her way.

"I haven't gotten used to the way your eyes glow when you are turned on. Dragons' eyes have a flame that burns in the center. Does this only happen with your mate or does it happen with any female?" Nate asked, breaking the moment.

"With anyone," Suvi responded, irritated at the interruption.

"Thank the Gods. I was worried for a minute. This female named Paula had glowing eyes the entire time she was talking to me and she is annoying as shit. All I could think was if your Goddess thought to make her my mate, I was slitting my throat. No way in hell was I going to spend five minutes with her, much less eternity."

"How the hell did Plain Paula get in? I specifically left her off the invite. I swear one day I'm going to turn her into a toad," Suvi vowed, trying to think of a way to get rid of the bothersome female before she started running of the guests.

Caine picked up her hand and kissed her knuckles, laughter dancing in his eyes. "My ferocious little mate. Forget about her, let's dance. It was good to talk to you, Nate.

Someday, I will take you up on your offer and visit Khoth to see your purple moon."

"Oooo, your realm has a purple moon? I wonder if that would impact our powers differently," Suvi postulated, excited by the prospect of visiting other realms and experimenting.

"You can talk moons and magic later, love. Right now you're all mine," Caine said, grabbing her hand, dragging her to the make-shift dance floor.

"Moons and magic, I like the sound of that. That could be the theme of our mating ceremony." Her wheels started spinning with all kinds of thoughts for the ceremony. First on her list was finding the perfect pair of shoes.

Caine pulled her close and began a slow dance despite the upbeat tempo of the music currently playing. "Speaking of our mating, I think we should do it on the full moon in a few days, rather than wait."

"That anxious to be mated to me?" she husked into his ear.

"You have no idea how anxious I am to be mated to you," he murmured, grabbing her ass and tugging her closer so she felt the hard line of his erection.

"Mmmm, I think I have some kind of idea. And, I really want this pain in my brand to end. It grates on my nerves, always keeping me on edge." She didn't mention the unsettling feeling she had in her gut that the rug was going to be pulled out from under them. Cele was out there and more pissed than ever. Suvi had no doubt that the High Priestess was going to retaliate in a big way.

"It's not the brand that is keeping you on edge. The unresolved threat is what's eating at you. At least we have each other now and nothing can keep us apart," Caine promised. She gazed into his green eyes and felt some of her worry seep away. He was right. They were stronger together which was why Cele had tried so hard to get rid of Caine before they could be joined.

Donovan's scream cut off that line of thought and had her turning around to see what was going on. Black smoke filled the air on the other side of the pool where Donovan was splashing and playing. She glanced to her sisters and saw Isis running to get her son. Suvi was in motion at the same time Pema was. Suvi searched the black smoke, expecting to see Cele, but didn't immediately see anyone. She remained on guard given that the smoke appeared the same as they'd encountered the night they had saved Donovan from Cele's grasp.

Malicious intent radiated from the smoke like a plague, seeking to infect anything it contacted. Caine latched onto her left hand at the same time she took Pema's. They halted at the side of the pool just as the smoke cleared, revealing a stunning female sorceress with dark brown hair. She recognized the mocha skin and eerie black eyes.

"Angelica," Jace hissed from close behind her. Hatred and contempt poured off the sorcerer in waves. Suvi and her sisters had helped Jace discover a spell that Angelica had cast on him during a time when the female had held him prisoner. This female had done unspeakable things to Jace, and in Suvi's opinion, was just as evil as Cele.

Isis reached back and touched Pema's arm, joining the three of them together, preparing to defend an attack, if necessary. Suvi glanced down and saw that Donovan was almost to the edge of the pool and still vulnerable.

"What do you want?" Zander demanded from a few feet away. Suvi glanced around and noted that most of their guests had retreated to the other side of the property. The sprites were flying frantically around the top of the barrier

Suvi had cast earlier. They zoomed around the balloons in their agitation, causing several to pop.

Angelica waltzed to the food table and picked up a truffle, popping it into her mouth. "I only want what is mine. Jace and the Mystik Grimoire. Relinquish them to me and I will leave peacefully."

"Over my dead body!" Jace yelled while shoving his mate behind him, shielding her with his body. "I'm not yours, Angelica. I never was and I never will be," Jace spat.

"As for the Grimoire," Zander interrupted, "you will never lay one hand on the tome. It would never allow it." Suvi had heard rumors about the magical book and its ability to appear and disappear. It contained prophecies, ancient spells, and knowledge about how to access any realm, which was no doubt why the female wanted to get her hands on it.

A dark light began to glow between Angelica's fingertips, alerting Suvi that she was about to attack. She squeezed Pema's hand. "Let's do a protection spell," she whispered.

Angelica's head swiveled in their direction as if she heard the soft-spoken words. Without hesitation Suvi and her sisters chanted, "*cosaint.*"

Angelica's rebuff was instantaneous. Black light left her hands and hit their barrier, sending sparks shooting into the air. Several balloons popped as the magic hit them while some of Angelica's spell seeped around the barrier before they had cast it. A couple of the band members cried out and collapsed against the floor. Zander and his Dark Warriors rushed to form a wall of muscle between the loose magic and the rest of their guests.

Suvi was about to rush to their side when Jace and Gerrick simultaneously called their staffs to them, dissipating the spell before anyone else fell to it. Feeling triumphant, Suvi turned back to smirk at the sorceress when her face fell. Angelica was laughing loudly as if she had been thwarted. Suvi glanced at her sisters silently asking if they understood. They both shook their heads in confusion.

Angelica's hand went behind her and then flung forward. Suvi's beloved lounge chairs went airborne. She had spent hours picking them out and they were about to be destroyed. She ducked as one went sailing over their heads and smashed against the wall of their house. Ronan roared and snatched one out of the air and tossed it aside, salvaging it. Zander was by his side in seconds as well as his Dark Warriors.

Isis crouched and pulled Donovan out of the water while the Vampire King and others kept them safe. "Run to Fen's hideaway," Isis instructed the little boy. Fen was at his side in seconds and Suvi saw the tale-tell signs of sprite magic surrounding her nephew. Confident that he would be safe, Suvi and her sister turned back to the battle at hand. Most of their guests were crouching and hiding anywhere they could while some of the braver ones fought back.

Isis screamed obscenities at the sorceress and picked up a tiki torch, throwing it at Angelica. She batted the torch aside and crouched low, muttering something in a language Suvi didn't recognize and spoke directly to Jace. "Jace, love, come with me. We belong together." Suvi could feel the power of the compulsion in the words and worried Jace would succumb.

Suvi chanced a glance at Jace. It was obvious the healer was affected, but he didn't give in. Angelica was furious and flinging every object within reach at them. Most ended up in their pool while others found their mark. It was chaotic as their guests dodged objects and tried to protect themselves.

The sprites joined the fight as well. Sprites were tiny creatures, but some of the most magical Fae in existence and fiercely loyal. Suvi saw Fen rush in, glowing bright red with her anger and clutching a tiny acorn in her hand. She tossed the acorn with greater force than Suvi had expected. A smile broke over Suvi's face as she watched the acorn hit its target and explode across the side of Angelica's face, leaving a bleeding divot in its wake. Dozens of sprites began hurtling tiny balls of fire at the sorceress, making her scream in frustration.

"This isn't over, Jace. I will have you," Angelica promised before disappearing in a puff of black smoke.

Cheers erupted from the crowd and a winded voice next to her had Suvi both cringing and smiling at the same time. "Wow! That was a killer workout. There's no telling how many calories I just burned dodging chairs. I'm going to have to add that to my work-out regimen," Plain Paula huffed.

"You do that Paula. I have a dance to finish," Suvi said, walking away.

"That female really is annoying," Caine observed from next to her.

"Yes she is." Suvi grabbed Caine's hand and walked over to her sisters.

"Check on the band and get them playing again, Suvi. Isis and I will get to work putting the furniture back in place," Pema instructed. "We aren't going to let her ruin our night."

As she glanced around, she could tell that no one was seriously injured and she was relieved. Hell no, they weren't going to let that evil bitch ruin their night. "Let's get this party started," Suvi called out to the guests, taking Caine and planting a kiss on his lips as the band started playing.

CHAPTER 8

"I suppose you guys aren't hanging around to help clean this mess up?" Pema asked Zander facetiously.

The Vampire King chuckled and slapped Pema on the shoulder. "No' on your life, lass, but feel free to put Nate to work. He needs to do something other than harass females. We need to talk aboot Angelica's appearance and I want Jace and Gerrick to cast the new layers of protection around your property that we have around Zeum."

"Yeah, there's a lot I could say about that female, but let's start with the obvious," Isis snarled. "Why in the hell did she barge into our party and how did she access the same dark magic Cele has? Sorcery and witchcraft are vastly different and don't tap into the same power source."

Caine understood little about witches and sorcerers, but he did know that witches used the power of the four elements while sorcerers shaped and wielded the magic of the earth. The way Suvi had explained it seemed like a matter of semantics to him, but then he was a vampire. One thing that was undeniable was that when he came into contact with the magic, he could feel the difference. When Jace and Gerrick had cast their spells during the party there was a dense, heavy atmosphere surrounding them whereas Suvi and her sisters' was lighter. It was as different as a light drizzle compared to a heavy rainfall.

"She barged into the party because she is a delusional nut-job," Jace answered, picking up empty cups and setting them on a table. "I felt the same power with Cele that night in the basement when we rescued Donovan."

"I doona think it is too much of a stretch to say that the archdemon, Kadir, gave them the power. I detected a scent that I have only smelled when I've been in his or other lesser demons' presence," Zander added.

"The real question is what goal the two females have in common," Suvi pointed out. "Angelica seems to have her sights fixed on Jace where Cele is focused on us, so what's the connection? You know her best, Jace. What do you think?" Caine watched Suvi wince and turn pale as if she regretted her words the moment they left her lips.

"Thankfully, I haven't seen or heard from her for six hundred years. The only thing she has ever wanted was more power and she felt the way to get that was through me and the Mystik Grimoire."

"Och, that's it, that's the connection. Kadir must be promising to give them more power," Zander interjected. "He is a sneaky mother-fucker playing on realm weaknesses. I'm no' worried aboot Angelica getting the Grimoire, the tome willna allow that. We need to find oot where these two females are and end them before they can do anymore damage. We need to expand patrols and pull double shifts to include daylight hours since the females are no' confined to the night. I willna allow my realm members and warriors to be targeted again."

"We can check with Trixie and ask if Cele has visited her shop recently. Cele wants to bring her daughter back and even if that's not possible, witches need supplies to perform their magic. She can't go back to her home or the academy, so she will need to get the items somewhere else," Pema added.

"What do we do if we encounter them? Both females are unstable and difficult to contain," Caine observed, hating the idea of his mate placing herself in a perilous situation.

"Yeah, you could say that. Angelica clearly lives in a delusional world and Cele is dangerous and very powerful," Isis said. "The three of us battled Cele and barely managed to hold her back. I don't know about Angelica's power, but I think it's safe to say if you find them, you shouldn't approach them without the three of us present. Our best bet of being able to beat either one of them is if Suvi completes her mating on the full moon in a couple of days." Caine had no doubt that Isis was right. He'd had a nagging suspicion that mating Suvi needed to happen soon and the episode tonight only confirmed it.

Still, Caine had to bite back his protective instincts that wanted to take Suvi away to a remote island where no one would ever find them and live happily ever after with no interference. But, she wasn't one to be shielded behind steel doors. She was a powerful witch who was destined to take over ruling the witches.

"Sounds like we have a mating to plan," Suvi said, nudging his side and bringing him out of his thoughts. He looked down at her and smiled broadly. Hell yeah, a mating ceremony sounded perfect. In the midst of all the craziness he had found himself embroiled in, why not add a little more chaos to the pot? Especially when it involved him and the hottest witch he'd ever laid eyes on. He was one lucky male.

CAINE PULLED his mate's sport car into his driveway, glad to be home. It had only been three days since Sally was murdered and yet it seemed like an eternity had passed. He shouldn't be surprised. After all, he faced and overcame a death sentence, found his Fated Mate, survived an attack from an evil sorceress, and so much more. The harrowed murder investigation, birthday party, and daytime outings (when he had never before gone out during the day) were all just icing on the cake. On the brink of becoming over-whelmed again, Suvi's soul caressed him from the inside. It set his fangs on edge with arousal and calmed him at the same time. And damn, if that didn't make his mate mark burn like the fires of hell.

He looked over at the female who had become his universe and was captured by her enticing, brown eyes. His gaze traveled over her face and down to the pulse in her neck. His hunger spiked as he saw the blood rushing in her veins. Her panting breaths made her chest heave up and down, drawing his attention. He licked his lips and imag-ined feasting on her luscious breasts. His eyes traveled to her long legs. She crossed them and he had to agree, the right shoes made all the difference when he saw his mate mark on her ankle. Her impossibly high-heels showcased his mark even more, leaving no doubt that she belonged to him. His entire body throbbed with need as every part of her inflamed him.

"So, this is where you live?" Suvi asked as they climbed out of the car and met his eyes over the roof. He heard the questions she didn't ask. *Are you expecting me to move in with you? Or, will you move in with me?*

He knew she wouldn't want to leave her sisters now, or at any time. And honestly, he would never ask her to. The three of them were more powerful together and shouldn't be separated. Sure he had his parents, but they traveled frequently and were rarely ever home. He hurried around the car and pulled her into his arms. "I live here with my parents. Although, most of the time they are traveling. Do you think your sisters would mind if my parents stayed with us at Casa de Rowan when they are in town?"

Her smile beamed so brightly, it could lighten the darkest night. "You really don't mind moving in with us? Do you think your parents will be okay with that? We can't leave them alone in this house. My dad never wanted to live with us and decided to move in with his sister and her family."

"Of course I'm moving in, where else would I be? My parents will love it, they've always wanted a bigger family, but haven't managed to get pregnant again."

"Oh, Caine. That's the best news I've heard all day. Your parents can have the room next to Donovan's," she said jumping into his arms.

He held her close and nuzzled her neck. "You know, things have happened so fast and we have been on a roller coaster since we met. It's nice to have a moment to breathe, despite the fact that we still have this urgent life and death matter hanging over us." He lowered his head, savoring the flare of her pupils and met her lips. The slightest contact with her mouth was like a match to tinder. He went up in flames and the kiss turned harsh and demanding, reflecting his need. It took every ounce of his formidable strength to pull out of the kiss.

She was breathing as heavy as he was and her heart

was pounding out a beat that matched his own. Her gorgeous, brown eyes glowed with her arousal. "I'm not so certain that we should let our guard down," she murmured, but her body was saying the complete opposite.

He placed kisses on the side of her throat and whispered in her ear, "We have tonight, love. Let's leave everything else for tomorrow." They weren't going to solve their problems in the next eight hours, but he could explore more of his luscious mate.

She leaned her head on his shoulder as they made their way into his house. "Cele is a loose cannon right now. She's lost too much to simply forget about us and disappear. That demon she is paired up with is a force we can't beat and who knows if she is partnering with Angelica, too. It will be safer if we get back to our place where the protections are in place. I can't lose you."

He rubbed her back, trying to comfort her. "You aren't going to lose me, I promise. We will be safe enough here for the next couple hours. You can cast a spell here to be extra certain."

She turned to face him and ran her hand up his chest. "What did you have in mind?" Her pulse quickened and his hunger slammed into him like a freight train. The taste of her blood mixed with her arousal was addicting and he needed more than the sample he had when they had made love.

His fangs descended and he clenched his teeth, breathing through his need. He planned on savoring his mate this time and that wouldn't happen if he gave into his needs this early. That plan nearly flew out the window when Suvi gazed at his mouth, her eyes becoming heavy-lidded. That fast, he was rock-hard. A moan slipped out when she swept her long, black hair aside, revealing her neck in wordless invitation.

He gave up holding back. They had eternity to do it nice and slow, he thought, as he gathered her soft curvaceous body into his arms and ran his tongue over her pulse. Imagining all the ways he would taste her, he sucked her flesh into his mouth and eased his fangs into the vein at her neck. The groan that escaped from her spoke of sex and surrender. The sound caressed his heated senses as her hot blood flowed into his mouth. She arched against him, pressing her breasts into his chest as she climaxed from his bite...the bite of a mate. Satisfaction at how easily he could bring her pleasure had him growling as he drank. Suddenly, it wasn't enough for him. He wanted her skin on his.

He continued taking what she so freely offered and impatiently reached up, ripping her shirt open down the front. Her bra became his next casualty and his hands were filled with lush breasts. The feel of her pearled nipples against his palm had his blood pumping south, lengthening his straining cock. In the excitement, he sucked hard at her neck. He let go of one of her breasts to grab her ass, pulling her roughly against his aching shaft.

He was overcome by a fierce need to possess her body, mind, and soul. His beast clawed to be let free, surprising him. He'd always believed himself a cultured male, above primal animal sex, but his witch had changed all that. He withdrew his fangs and didn't swipe his tongue over the twin pinpricks, preferring to watch blood trickle down her neck and shoulder blade.

"Clothes off, now," she demanded, clawing at his shirt.

"I lose my mind when I touch you, love. You sure you're ready for me?" He drew his shirt over his head and tossed it aside.

"You aren't ready for me, baby. I'm going to eat you alive," she cooed at him. Her smile was downright salacious. She walked backwards, pulling him into his living room while unbuttoning his pants. Frantically, she unzipped them and stopped in her tracks when his shaft sprang free. He watched her stare at his erection and then drop to her knees. His mind went crazy with fantasies about what he wanted to do with her. He tested their mental pathway and sent her the images.

"Mmmm, I like the way you think. Where to start?" she wondered aloud. Her hand was bold in its approach and gripped his thick erection firmly. Fuck, he'd never had a female so aggressive before and it felt so damn good. She positioned him before her mouth and he lost his breath at the intense look on her face. She was the most amazing female he had ever seen as she took his cock into her mouth. There was no shy hesitation. She was sure and skilled as she licked the head like an ice cream.

"Goddess, baby. Suck me hard. All the way to the back of your throat," he ordered. She didn't hesitate to oblige his request, sucking him so hard all rational thought splintered. There was only her hot mouth and heaven as he gripped her hair, pumping into her. She sucked then swallowed, taking more of his length and his control. He pulled at her silken lengths. "Stop, baby. I'm not going to last."

An incoherent mumble was her only reply as she continued her ministrations. He jerked his hips back and his cock popped out of her mouth. He couldn't take another second. He pushed his jeans down and off, then rid her of her remaining clothing as well. "My turn," he growled and picked her up, setting her down on the back of his sofa.

He spread her legs and settled on his knees in front of her, exposing her core to his gaze. He ran one finger through her velvet soft petals, relishing the slick evidence of her arousal. She glistened in the low lighting. He leaned in and took her mouth in a fierce kiss as he plunged two fingers into her molten core. She was so tight, hot and wet for him.

He kissed a path down her neck, licking the blood that had trailed down from his bite. He paused to pay attention to each of her lush, full breasts, sucking one peak into his mouth, laving the stiff bud.

She groaned and fisted his black hair. He loved how she held him to her body. He licked from her breast down her abdomen. He paid special attention to her navel before running his fangs lightly over her skin down to her black curls. He recalled how much she liked when he bit her intimate flesh.

His tongue took time to lap up her juices as he decided where to strike. His fingers continued to slide in and out of her body while he focused on her clit. He teased the little bundle of nerves and slowly pierced it with his fangs. Immediately, she detonated with another orgasm. His cock ached to be inside her.

He pulled his fingers out and rested his head on her lower stomach, fighting to cage the beast and regain control. Deep breathing only took her melon scent further into his lungs and fanned the flames. He made his way up to her face and touched his wet lips to hers. He curled his tongue between her lips with a sensual tenderness that poured all of his immeasurable care and profound emotion for her.

Impatiently, she reached down, taking his cock and rubbing it through her slick channel. The beast was roaring for release again and he slammed into her in one brutal stroke. He gripped the back of her neck and thrust into her with abandon. She clawed his back and held on as he pounded into her. She was perched on the back of the couch and his entire being was focused on the friction between their bodies, driving him rapidly to the edge.

Her muscles flexed and tightened around his shaft. She licked the sweat beading on his chest and sucked one of his nipples into her mouth. He cried out, loving the way she played his body. "Fucking hell," he cursed, holding her hips as he fucked her with all his strength. She screamed his name as she climaxed, triggering his own. He thrust into her one last time and poured his hot seed into her womb. He dropped his head to her shoulder as his orgasm raged on. This was his mate, the one who completed him.

"Goddess, will we ever make it to a bed?" she teased and kissed his temple.

His climax had yet to end, but the thought of taking her in his bed had him picking her up and walking down the hall.

SUVI HAD NEVER FELT BETTER in her life. Caine had just fucked her into oblivion on his couch and was now driving her to climax once again as he walked down the hall while still inside of her. He captured her mouth and she slid her tongue along his. He was an aphrodisiac, ramping up her desire, despite the three orgasms she'd already had. She ground her pelvis against him, making his steps falter.

"Watch it, minx. I want to make love to you in my bed this time."

"I can't" she nipped his neck, "help myself. You drive me crazy and I'm going to cum again." She writhed wantonly, taking what she wanted from him. He paused in the hall to lean her against the wall and take her again. Her body tingled, signaling her climax.

"That's it, baby. Take what you need." He knew how to move his body in all the right ways and before she knew it, she was coming apart at the seams. She threw her head back and called out his name to the heavens. "You are so beautiful when you cum in my arms," he murmured.

Her eyes were still closed when he was in motion again, heading into a large bedroom. His movement in and out of her while he walked was erotic as hell and she was infinitely grateful he was a supernatural, capable of taking her all night long because she was nowhere near done with him. She intentionally squeezed her inner muscles, gripping his length even tighter.

He gasped and dropped her to the bed. "You will pay for that." He came down over the top of her and placed a gentle, loving kiss on her collarbone. She reached between them hating the separation from him. She closed her hand around his velvety broad tip and stroked him while she rolled him over with her free hand. He obliged her and went to his back. She sat up and straddled his waist, kissing the bulges and hollows of his chest. One of her hands snaked around her back and found his sac. His testicles were drawn up tight underneath him and she caressed the heavy round globes. His hips left the bed and pushed his thick shaft against her core.

She lifted up and positioned him so that his thick head breached her core. He bared his fangs at her. His fierce beauty stole her heart as he gripped her hips and thrust into her with savage need. She braced herself with her palms on his chest muscles.

"Hold on tight, big guy. This is my game now," she warned with a smile.

CHAPTER 9

Water dripped somewhere in the back of the cave, agitating Cele even more, if that was possible. Frustrated, she stooped down, picked up a rock and threw it into the dark recesses. She paced, hovering close to the fire she had conjured. The damp cold of the cave seeped into her bones, making her shiver. To top off her crappy day, the fire flickered and went out. The complete darkness didn't faze her as she whipped her wand out, pointing it at the pile of wood. "*Dóiteáin*," she muttered. An orange flame shot from the tip and rekindled the flame.

Her thoughts were whirling through her head. Her plan for Suvi's mate to be executed had failed and she had no doubt those pretentious witches were planning a mating at that very moment. She had trusted that Angelica would stick to their plan of weakening the witches, so she'd given her the location of their home, but that ungrateful sorceress had used the opportunity for another attempt at her endgame. Of course, Angelica had failed because she'd gone in half-cocked and allowed her emotions to dictate her actions.

Cele had told her to eliminate one of the Rowan sisters' mates. She didn't even have to target Caine. At this point, any of the males would do. The point was to weaken the sisters and force them to relinquish their power to her. Had she done her part, Cele would have ensured Angelica had her sorcerer, as well as, the Mystik Grimoire. Now, the Rowans had probably linked the final couple, reinforcing their defenses.

A red haze covered her vision when she thought about how those triplets had thwarted her and now had possession of her beloved daughter. She didn't care that they had the vampire. She had made sure that any foray into his mind would kill him. Otherwise, she was going to have to deal with him sooner or later. What had her blood boiling and losing sight of reason was that they had Claire, and Goddess only knew what they were doing to her.

There wouldn't be anywhere those triplets could hide if they decided to cremate her daughter. That was the only state the demon told her from which her daughter couldn't return. She needed to get her back so the demon could fulfill his end of the bargain and return her to the living. Having Claire back had become as important as garnering the Rowan sisters' powers.

Now, all she had to do was get into Zeum and steal the amulet and her daughter. Once she had Claire back, together they would find a way to get the power of three for their own. She silently cursed losing the vampire so soon. He may have disclosed the location of Zeum, but she had no idea what type of protections and security they had in place. No doubt it was extensive, involving every type of magic the realm had to offer. She'd approach the compound at night when most of the warriors were out on patrol.

A thought struck her. If Zander and the Dark Warriors were at the Rowan's party then they could be working together and were likely out searching for her and Angelica. She could use that, lay a false trail. If she made a golem using her hair and blood, she could lure the Vampire King and most of the others away from Zeum, providing the best opportunity. She wondered if she should ask Angelica for the assistance of her subjects since Cele had alienated everyone at the academy.

She stopped her pacing, satisfied that her plan would work. Even without Angelica's help, she had everything she needed to get that amulet and her daughter. She was the most powerful witch ever created, and she had been brave enough to welcome the forbidden power, making her magic unbeatable. She turned and another wave of her wand had a glowing sphere floating before her, lighting her way out of the cave. Increasing her footsteps, she was glad to put the cavern behind and with each step she became more excited. Soon she would have the amulet and her daughter, and no one would stop Kadir from bringing Claire back from the dead.

CAINE FOLLOWED his mate down the hall as she headed to the back of their house. His gaze was riveted to her firm ass as it swayed provocatively before him. It had only been minutes since he had last had her, but he needed her again. The memory of how she had ridden him had a groan escaping his throat.

"I know, baby. We need to plan our ceremony with my

sisters and then we can escape again. We have to get mated on the next full moon so we are strong enough to beat Cele," she assured him. The way she had turned to look at him, fidgeting with a pink button at the top of her shirt distracted him to no end. The button-down was tight across her breasts and the button was calling his name.

Drawn to her like iron to a magnet, he reached out and popped the top one free, exposing more of her creamy flesh. His finger tip traced the curve of her ample bosom and then dipped inside her bra to tease her pert nipple. His fangs descended, her sweet melon taste still on his tongue intensified with her responding arousal.

She stepped into his body and placed her hands on his hips. His free hand took hold of her backside, pulling her even closer. His shaft was hard as steel and their clothing was a flimsy barrier. He could feel her heat surround him and he throbbed in response. He knew he should pull back and had every good intention to meet with her sisters, but desire won out and his mouth came crashing down on hers. He kissed her roughly, and things quickly got carried away. His hand was under her cotton skirt and grasping the firm flesh of her ass.

A small laugh broke the moment and Suvi quickly pulled away from him, straightening her shirt and tugging on her skirt. He saw the young stripling with his soft brown curls and mischievous smile. Caine couldn't help but notice the curious look in the male's eyes. Suvi reached down and ruffled his hair. "What's up, D? Where is everyone?" She glanced toward Caine, her cheeks flushed with embarrassment and desire. Stunning, sexy, and deliciously captivating.

"They're waiting for you in the kitchen. They ordered Chinese. You're always kissing Caine. I thought it was me and you against the world, Aunt Suvi." The little guy tilted his head adorably and Caine couldn't get angry over the possessive nature of his words.

Suvi laughed and leaned down next to the stripling. "You know he's my Fated Mate, but you're still my best buddy. And, it will always be you and me against that growly bear."

Caine stepped next to his mate and wrapped his arm around her waist. He felt a surge in power like he did when they had joined at Marshall's house. He wondered how much more that would increase once they were fully mated. "I have a feeling that you two will cause a lot of trouble. I hope for the sake of peace in this house that you two take pity on the poor bear."

"What do you do? And, are you moving in here, too?" Donovan asked imperiously.

Caine couldn't stop the smile that broke across his face. This little guy was going to be formidable. "I work with money. I help supernaturals make more and keep what they have." Caine looked at Suvi and got caught in her brown eyes for several long moments. He had witnessed the closeness between her and her sisters and he could see how much she had come to mean to this little stripling. "Yes, I am moving in and my parents will stay here sometimes. That makes us family now."

Donovan cocked his head and thought over what Caine had told him. "So, I'll have more grandparents then," he said excitedly. "Ones that will live with me. I bet they'll spoil me rotten." They all laughed at that. Donovan would have his parents wrapped around his little finger from the moment they met.

Suvi grabbed his hand and began walking down the hall. Donovan followed suit and grabbed Suvi's other hand, reminding Caine that she was his, too. "Do you think I will have a little brother or sister soon? Or, maybe you or Pema will have a baby. Then I wouldn't be the only kid here. That would be awesome."

Caine's steps faltered and his heart began racing in his chest. A child. He had never thought of having a family of his own. It wasn't until recently that the Goddess started blessing Fated Mates again. Suvi tugged on his hand and smirked at the alarm on his face.

"I think you need to tell your dad that you want a little sister. Isis would love to give you one," Suvi responded. "And," she said, keeping her eyes locked with Caine's, "you will have cousins as soon as possible. Caine and I are trying hard to make a baby. Aren't we, sweetheart?" She winked at him and his heart began racing once again in panic.

Isis and Pema began laughing as they had entered the kitchen. Caine felt sweat break out on his forehead and he had trouble breathing on top of his already pounding heartbeat. "Planning on striplings already, little sister," Pema teased. "Is that why Caine is sweating?"

"That's cause he's been working so hard making a baby with Aunt Suvi," Donovan supplied helpfully.

Braeden scooped up his son and laughed. "Is that so? Do you want some fried rice?"

"Yes, please. And, daddy, I want a baby sister. Aunt Suvi said you and mommy will give me one."

"The Goddess decides who has babies. We will all have children when she deems it right," Isis told the little guy as she dished up some food for him. Braeden set him down and he ran eagerly to the table. Everyone crowded around the spread of take-out with Donovan. Emotion clogged Caine's throat at the feeling of belonging to this family. He had been blessed beyond anything he'd ever imagined.

"Can I be in your mating ceremony? Dad said I did a

great job in his and I already know what to do," Donovan asked excitedly as he shoveled rice into his mouth. More food fell off his spoon than made it into his mouth, leaving a pile around his place setting. Caine couldn't help but grin and hand the young boy a napkin.

The aroma of soy sauce and ginger had Caine's stomach growling. He grabbed two plates and handed one to Suvi who was answering Donovan. "I would love for you to be in our ceremony and I have the perfect job for you. Can you be in charge of holding our mating stone until we need it? It's a huge responsibility. Do you think you're up for it?"

Donovan sat up higher in his chair and thrust his chin up. "Oh, yes, Suvi. I'll guard it with my life. You can count on me. I even have a special box where it will be safe."

"Are you planning on completing the ceremony in two days?" Ronan asked. The big bear had on a black tank top with the Confetti Too logo across the chest and tattered jeans. The male was one of the biggest bouncers Caine had ever seen and he understood why Killian had hired him at the club. And, it wasn't just because he was a bear shifter. He looked more like one of the Dark Warriors. Caine would never fuck with him that was for sure. Not that he couldn't hold his own, but he wasn't a stupid male.

"Yeah. There is no way we're going to wait. Cele is going to make her move soon, I can feel it. She is desperate and desperation makes people stupid. Plus, my brand is killing me. I don't know how either one of you managed to live with the pain for so long." At the mention of their mating marks, his gave an answering throb as Suvi met his eyes. He once again felt the urgency to fully claim her, his fangs pressing against his lower lip.

"The Vampire King has agreed to perform the ceremony the night after tomorrow. What else can I do to help? I'm not any good at planning parties, but give me a task and point me in the right direction and I'm fine," he said and ate a bite of some Kung Pao Chicken.

Suvi squeezed his thigh before digging into her own plate of food. "You need to get your tux for the ceremony and you two need to go shopping for a dress with me in the morning," Suvi told her sisters around a bite of her egg roll. "I know that I don't have time to have Beladora create a one of a kind masterpiece, but she makes the best dresses so I'm sure she has something that will make me look stunning."

He was stunned that his mate didn't know how extraordinary she was. She didn't need a special dress to make her gorgeous. She made cut-off jeans and torn t-shirts look good.

"Where are you going to have the ceremony? Here or Zeum?" Isis asked, dipping her wanton in chili sauce.

Caine thought about that. He didn't doubt that Zander would allow them to have the ceremony at Zeum, but that somehow didn't feel right to him. "I think we should have it here. This is where we will make our life with your sisters and I can't think of a better location," he replied.

"The tables are all still out back from your birthday," Donovan shared helpfully.

"You're right," Isis responded to her step-son and ruffled his hair. "You can help me clean out the pool later today."

Donovan clapped happily about his role and Caine listened as Suvi and her sisters planned every last detail as he texted Zander telling him where the ceremony was going to be. Suvi's soul stirred in his chest as the pieces began to fall into place. It didn't matter that he had known them for just a short amount of time. They had come to mean the world to him.

CHAPTER 10

"**M**ove that comb over. It doesn't look right there," Pema told Isis. Suvi watched in her mirror as they argued over her hair. A flock of butterflies had taken flight in her stomach and she was giddy with joy that her moment was finally here. It didn't matter that she was only twenty-eight years old because she felt all of Caine's three hundred fifty years of waiting through their bond.

She'd hardly slept after they had finished making all the plans. Her sisters had gone with her to visit Beladora where she found a crystal-encrusted work of art. The strapless dress hugged her body from her chest to her ankles and every inch was covered with beads and pearls. Despite being off the rack, it was perfect.

She'd had more trouble finding the right shoes and had spent most of yesterday hopping from store to store. Finally, at the last stop she found a pair of Louboutin's that were to die for. The brilliant red soles caught her eye immediately, but it was the crystal-embellished suede pumps that took her shoe fetish to a whole new level. The ladylike peep toe, the studded-all over crystals, and the six-inch heel...oh my! While she may have fallen in love with Caine, a female could fall in love with shoes, too, right? They'd cost her as much as the dress, but she had to have them. And for once, her sisters had agreed with her on the perfection of her choice in footwear.

She was anxious about leaving the final set-up and arrangements to Courtney and the sprites. She was typically the one to put the final stamp on everything, and this, of all nights, mattered most to her, but they had promised her they wouldn't disappoint. She took a deep breath, reassuring herself that this was going to be perfect.

Her thoughts jumped to a bigger issue that had been lingering in the back of her mind all day. She knew there were plenty of protections in place and prayed that neither Angelica nor Cele got as much as one hair through their barriers.

A knock at the door interrupted and their mother poked her head around the door. "Everyone is ready and waiting for you. Oh, sweetie, you look beautiful!" Their mother cooed, rushing to her side and drawing her in for a big hug.

"Thanks, mom. How's dad?" Suvi asked. Their father had had a difficult time when their mother left him after she'd found her Fated Mate. They had been together for centuries. Suvi had to believe he would find his Fated Mate and happiness someday. She was glad that Braeden's brother had taken him under his wing in his construction business, giving their father a new start.

"Your dad is beaming with pride and I swear I saw tears in his eyes, but don't tell him I told you that. I'll tell them five more minutes," their mother said as she kissed her cheek and turned around to look at her sisters. "I have the most beautiful daughters in the Tehrex Realm. And, I'm not just saying that because I'm your mom," she croaked, her eyes filling with tears.

Pema crossed to their mom and drew her into a hug. "Thanks, mom. Go tell dad that Suvi will be out shortly." Suvi was so glad to see that her sister had repaired her relationship with their mother. There had been a time after their mom's mating that Pema refused to speak to her and wouldn't even be in the same room as their mom. Pema had harbored hatred toward their mother for causing their father so much pain when she left, but after she found her own mate, she understood the dynamics of the mating compulsion, and eventually forgave her.

As their mom left the room, Isis looked Suvi over. "Little bit more lip gloss," Isis observed and took out the tube and swiped more of the sticky substance across her lips. "Okay, now you're perfect."

Suvi smiled up at her sister, stood up and walked over to the full-length mirror. She gazed at her reflection with satisfaction. "With this dress and these shoes, it would be hard not to look amazing," she replied, turning to see the side view. The sparkle and shine of her dress and shoes made her burst with excitement.

She'd imagined this day since she was a little girl and every time she'd thought about it there had always been glitter, glam and high-heels. The fact that her sisters, her parents and all the people that mattered most were there to share this day meant the world to her. Not to mention that she was mating the male of her dreams. She was bubbling over with anticipation as she turned back to her sisters.

"Ready?" Pema smiled and grabbed her hand. Suvi felt the stone that was now embedded into her sister's palm. Isis grabbed her other hand and she felt her stone, as well. She would have one in her palm soon. A symbol of the completion of her mating and the strength of her power. Their collective power flared, making the lights flicker and energy fizzed through her veins. This was the crux of who they were...the power of three.

"I couldn't be more ready," she declared, smiling at them both.

"This is going to be one hell of a party," Isis crooned as she followed Suvi to the backyard. Her sister wasn't wrong about that.

Their father was waiting for her in the kitchen and her mother had been right. There was the tell-tale sheen to his eyes. "You look perfect, Sweetpea," he told her as he carefully kissed her cheek.

"Thanks, daddy. You look pretty spiffy yourself. All the females will swoon over you tonight." Their father blushed and she had to admit that he was a great-looking male with his dark-brown hair and green eyes. He was quite the catch, in her opinion.

"You are beautiful, too, Pumpkin," he said, giving Pema a kiss on the cheek. "And, you too, Hurricane," he added, giving Isis a kiss on the cheek, as well. Suvi smiled at the nickname he had given Isis at birth. His term of endearment had come from Isis' command of any room. Their parents had always told them that, even from birth, Isis had the attention of everyone around her. Over the years, the term came to mean more as they came to understand her ability to absorb the emotions of others and it was an even more perfect fit.

"Love you, too, dad. See you out there, Suvi," Isis said as she headed out the door.

"Remember to breathe," Pema uttered the last bit of advice before she was gone.

"C'mon, baby girl, your mate has been waiting long

enough for you." She turned to her father and managed a nod before he took her arm. She stepped into the backyard and immediately her gaze traveled to the gazebo and stopped when she saw Caine. He was standing with Zander in the middle of their deck and, he was, simply put, breathtaking.

She didn't see the many friends and family that had gathered around, consumed as she was by the sight of Caine in a three piece black tuxedo. He was undoubtedly the best looking male on the planet. His black hair fell into his green eyes. He rocked the scruffy hair with the immaculate Armani suit. He smiled when he saw her and everything in her settled into place. This was where she was meant to be, with this male.

Her legs were shaking as her father walked her toward her future. Electricity arched between them the moment her dad put her hand into Caine's. She kissed her dad's cheek and saw one tear had fallen from his eye. He averted his gaze and quickly retreated.

Her heart raced with her anticipation. This was the moment she had been waiting for. Caine shared a knowing look with her before they turned to face Zander. Only then did she realize that the Vampire King was dressed in a Scottish kilt. The outfit would have looked comical on anyone but this male. On him, and his brothers, she conceded, it was anything but a skirt. On them, the black and grey Scottish finery screamed masculinity.

"Friends, and family, please form a circle around the couple," Zander instructed. Caine's mother smiled at her as she stepped up beside them. She had met her and his father the night before and had instantly loved them. And, Ellis and Ava had come bearing gifts for Donovan, proving that they were indeed going to spoil him rotten. Her sisters, their mates and their parents, along with Donovan, completed their inner circle. Braeden's brother, Griffin, and their parents, along with the Dark Warriors, comprised the next circle. She was pleasantly surprised to see Nate and Angus at the ceremony. Nate winked at her, making her smile.

Once the circles were formed and all had joined hands, the ceremony commenced. Zander cleared his throat and Suvi wondered if he was nervous. He had only performed one other ceremony, for Jace and his mate. "We have gathered here to join these individuals, under the eye of the Sun and the glow of the Moon. Let the circle be blessed and consecrated with Fire and Water." Zander motioned to her sisters.

Pema and Isis pointed their wands at the concrete and both chanted, "*Dóiteáin.*" A blaze encircled them and the fire rose from the earth to the heavens, concealing them from their guests. Through the flames, Suvi watched, as with a flourish, her sisters pointed their wands at the pool and chanted, "*Uisge.*" A fine mist of water rose from the nearby swimming pool to flow around the outskirts of the fire. With a flick of their wrists, the mist blew inward, extinguishing the fire.

Zander continued the ceremony. "We call to the Goddess Morrigan, and invoke her to bless this mating." He paused and raised his hands to the full moon above. Suvi could feel the Goddess' presence in the air around them, despite her absence. She'd heard that she had made an appearance at Zander's mating and wondered what that must have been like. Part of her was relieved the Goddess didn't show up at all the ceremonies because she was nervous as it was, and if she had shown up, Suvi may have passed out from hyperventilating.

"We call upon the spirits of the East, of Air, Spring and

new beginnings. We call upon the spirits of the South and the inner Fire of the Sun, Summer and personal will. We call upon the spirits of the West, of Water, Autumn, and healing and dreaming. We call upon the spirits of the North, of Earth, Winter, and the time of cleansing and renewal. Join us to bless this couple with your guidance and inspiration," Zander recited. Emotion choked Suvi while magic enveloped her and Caine. She watched love for her swell in Caine's eyes and she allowed her own feelings to be seen in her brown depths.

Zander turned to Donovan. "You have the stone, lad?" He ruffled her nephew's hair.

Donovan lifted an intricately carved wooden box and held it up. "Yes, sir. It's in here, safe and sound," he said proudly.

Zander opened the lid and removed the ordinary rock. He placed it in her hand then wrapped Caine's hand around hers, both surrounding the stone. Caine grabbed her left hand and placed it on his chest, over his heart, then placed his left hand over hers.

"I bless this mating under the Sun and the Moon. This circle of love and honour is open and never broken, so may it be," Zander's voice resonated with his blessing.

Heat built in the stone as she felt both souls leave her body to enter the stone. A brilliant green light flashed between their fingers and her skin tingled with the magic, automatically absorbing some of the energy. The connection she felt to Caine intensified, and she could now see the bond between them. A million golden threads wrapped around her heart and ran to his, entwining them. Their combined souls surged back into her body at that moment and she knew right away that she would carry part of Caine with her for all time. She was aware of his thoughts, every naughty one, as well as, the love he felt for her.

Her sisters had told her that she would feel complete in a way she'd never been before, but the reality of it was so much more than that, and yet, beyond explanation. What she didn't expect was the fulfillment of her full magic. She finally understood the prophecy and how it could be believed that she and her sisters would reform the face of witchcraft. The power coursing through her veins was that staggering. It was pure and untainted and so strong that it couldn't be contained within one being. She glanced briefly to her sisters and knew they had felt the same thing with her being the third and final piece to their puzzle.

She was prepared for the pain when it hit, but it still took her breath and had her heart racing. Caine had been warned about what would happen with their stone and kept hold of her hand, initiating their mental link. *I'm here with you, love. It will pass.* She felt him wrap her in his embrace as the light flared, then subsided. The pain subsided, leaving behind all the tender emotions she had come to discover since meeting Caine.

She heard the Goddess' voice whisper in her head. "*No power, not even death, can ever sever this bond. Mating stones protect and bless different aspects for different couples. Yours blesses and protects your magical power. The time to fulfill your prophecy is near. It will require the power of six to beat your enemy.*" Suvi was right about her reaction when she began having difficulty breathing. The Goddess was in her head and she couldn't form a single thought to reply to her. She heard a tinkling of laughter and the Goddess was once again speaking. "*Don't worry, I know.*"

A sense of calm spread through her body and she knew the Goddess was the reason. Suvi took a deep breath and allowed her curiosity to win out as she raised one, and then all, of her fingers. A beautiful emerald was embedded into her palm. It matched her vampire's eyes. She looked up and into those emerald depths. Heat was blazing back at her. It was going to be a long party, she thought, as Zander completed the ceremony.

CAINE GAZED at his Fated Mate, unable to believe that he was about to complete the final phase of his mating. It had taken every ounce of his will-power to hold back during the ceremony. He appreciated the need for the blessings, but the dress Suvi wore fit like a second skin and he'd wanted to peel it from her body the second she'd walked out of the backdoor with her father. All he could do was watch the hypnotic sway of her hips as she walked toward him. Desire, hot and hard, exploded throughout his entire body.

The moment her father had placed her hand in his, the electrical current that passed between them had turned him into a creature made up solely of base needs. His saving grace had been that he had something else to focus on and that was their mating ceremony. Even now, he still felt like he was in a dream. He couldn't believe that he had found his Fated Mate and was about to complete the blood exchange to fully make her his for eternity.

He finished unzipping her dress and slid it off her body. It fell to the floor in a pool at her feet. He ran a finger down her spine, enjoying the way she shivered under his touch. She wasn't wearing a bra and he had her stepping out of her white, lace thong in the next breath. His witch was standing before him naked as the day she was born, but for her remarkable shoes, and she was nothing short of exquisite.

He turned her to face him and she looked up at him through her thick, black lashes.

He reached up and took the silver combs from her hair, letting the long, black tresses cascade in waves down her back. His gaze traveled over her and stopped on her lush breasts which jutted invitingly. He cupped one in his hand and gave it a squeeze.

"I need you naked, mate," she murmured as she reached for the buttons on his shirt.

He let go of her breast and opened his pants while she worked on removing his shirt. The second his zipper was down, his erect cock sprang free, aching and full. Her eyes dipped to his shaft and she licked her lips and groaned aloud. Impatient, she yanked his shirt open, causing buttons to fly in every direction. He let the ruined cloth slide off his arms.

Her fingers sank into the flesh of his chest as he explored her breasts, tweaking and teasing her nipples. The way she arched into his touch was so uninhibited and raw that it robbed him of breath. She had no problem taking what she wanted from him or letting him know what she liked. It was rare in his experience for a female to be so bold with her desires and it was one more thing he loved about her.

She pushed his pants down and before he could step out of them, her hands were all over his body. He chuckled and pulled her close, meshing their bodies together.

"Is there something you want, love?" he asked, teasing her.

"Yes. I want all of you...inside me," she hissed. "Don't you want to taste my blood again?" She knew exactly how to bring him to his proverbial knees. His fangs filled his mouth and he hungered for a taste of her melon-sweet blood.

"More than anything," he answered honestly as she

twined her arms around his neck and pulled him down to her mouth.

He went willingly and at the first touch of their lips, he lost all thought. She traced her tongue along his lower lip and took advantage when he opened at the request. Suvi ran her tongue along his teeth, exploring, learning him. She paused at one of his fangs and ran her tongue along its length. His beast was rising and his groan of pleasure was ripped from him as the sensation went straight to his cock. It felt like she was licking his shaft. She shifted her attention to his other fang and he felt them lengthen with her strokes until they were at fully extended. He had never been so close to orgasm from someone licking his fangs. Of course, he had never experienced half of what she was putting his body through.

He took command of the kiss and slid his tongue along the rim of her lips, sucking on the bottom lip. Her moan of pleasure echoed his and arousal intensified her melon scent. She was ready for him. He hoped she was always this affected by him after they'd been together for centuries.

He reached between them and found her moist center. She was so fucking wet and hot and needy. She whimpered as he fingered her bundle of nerves and cupped one breast. Her moans were the sweetest sound, and the knowledge that he was the musician made his cock throb with frantic need. He wanted to savor this experience. After all, they would never have another blood exchange like this one, but when he slid one finger into her wet pussy, the only coherent thought he had was to sink into her tight sheath and take her blood.

With single minded determination, he guided her toward the bed. Their silhouettes danced across the wall of the candle-lit room. He lowered her onto the soft mattress and followed her down. Leaning on one elbow, he looked down, pausing long enough to appreciate the site before him. He caught a glimpse of her glistening flesh before he plunged home in one fierce stroke.

"Fuck!" he groaned. She was so tight and hot that he had to grit his teeth or lose control. She writhed under him and he had to grab her hips to still them. "Give me a minute, love. I want this to last longer than a handful of minutes. You feel too good." He pulled out slowly and thrust back in to her welcoming sheath.

"You don't have to worry about lasting that long," she moaned. "From the moment I saw you tonight, I've been aching for you. I won't last long, either," she panted. He gave into her demands and slowly pulled out, shoving harder and deeper this time.

"Damn, baby." That fast, he felt her muscles clench and ripple around his length. He increased his pace and the power behind his strokes. "We do the blood exchange now. I can't wait, and after this, I plan to have you all night long," he said against the pounding pulse in her neck.

"You have me forever," she promised.

His teeth sank into her artery and she detonated around him. His balls drew up tight, ready to explode. Her blunt little teeth ravaged his neck and the sharp pain was eclipsed by the ecstasy of his own orgasm. The sensation of his blood joining hers to make her fully his, set off another release before the first had even waned.

She took advantage of his bliss and flipped him onto his back. She lifted his hands and muttered, "*Go ceangal.*" Instantly, his wrists were magically bound to the bed posts. As she took over their love making, he was consumed with the thought that if he died and went to *Annwyn* at that moment, he would die a happy male.

CHAPTER 11

Caine stood with Braeden and Ronan in a remote section of the woods on the east side of the lake. Suvi and her sisters were bathed in the powerful light of the moon. After having swept the area with a besom, the witches placed several items on the cherry wood table that served as their altar. A trio of white candles carved with runes, along with a ceremonial athame, were precisely positioned. A scattering of colored crystals followed suit. Each of the sisters lit one of the candles and then Pema grabbed the bowl of salt and dried lavender from Suvi. Snakes writhed in Caine's gut...they were ready to cast the circle. He'd never witnessed the intricacies of doing extensive magic and he had been entranced until he realized they were going to begin.

He hadn't agreed with calling Cele to them so soon. He wanted to wait another century. They had only been mated the night before and he found it impossible to remain calm, but there was no backing out now. He silently cursed that he kept allowing his thoughts to go down that particular rabbit hole. He had been lectured that any negative energy would only taint the space and could alter their spell. The last thing he wanted was for them to call the hordes of hell to them. He reminded himself that he appreciated taking the offensive with Cele and they were doing this on their terms. It was the best way of facing her without her archdemon and sorceress cohorts.

Caine came to attention when Suvi grabbed his hand and moved him south of the altar. "Okay, babe. We are going to cast our circle now and then it will be show time. I need you with me," Suvi informed him with a smile and the turned to her sisters. "Ready?"

"It's now or never," Isis replied with determination. Each of the sisters took their mates' hands. Caine could feel the power build and gazed around their circle, noting the sisters were confident and competent which set him more at ease.

"Now remember, this is how we will be most powerful, so don't get any ideas about funny business," Pema teased her mate.

"Mate, I never stop having naughty thoughts about you. Now will be no different," Ronan growled. Caine happened to agree with the male. It was going to be difficult to watch Suvi perform this ritual naked and not ravage her. Unfortunately, there was nothing that was going to stop the fantasies.

Suvi smiled at him knowingly as she removed her green, silk robe. Caine was captivated by his mate as her nudity hit him like a punch in the gut. Suvi had explained that witches performed magic best when sky-clad to draw energy from the moon. She had also told him that they performed strong magic when sexual elements were involved and that she needed him to send that energy her way. He felt like he was throwing off so much sexual energy at the moment that they should be able to bring back that dead chick, Claire.

He found himself praying that they needed to act out his fantasies to add even more power to this ritual. He had never been an exhibitionist and believed what he and his mate did should stay between them, but he wouldn't hesitate to take her right there in front of her family.

He barely noticed the others remove their robes, but once they had all shed their respective robes, Pema began casting the circle. He watched in fascination as she took the salt mixture and walked deosil in a perfect circle. After she had completed her first circuit, white light emanated from the salt. On her second circuit, she began chanting, "I cast this circle to keep us free of all energies that are not of the Light," she glanced back and winked at Ronan.

Pema resumed her chant, "I allow within this circle only the energies that are of the Light. So mote it be." On her third walk around Caine listened as she consecrated the space and marveled at how powerful their witchcraft was. As a vampire, he had powers and abilities that were tied to the blood and the moon whereas his mate's was tied to the earth and the moon. He thought they complimented one another perfectly.

Isis proceeded to scribe the pentacle in salt, and invoked the element in each direction as she went. "Hear me, Sentinels of the East, We summon the powers of Air! Hear me, Sentinels of the South, We summon the powers of Fire! Hear me, Sentinels of the West, We summon the powers of Water! Hear me, Sentinels of the North, We summon the powers of Earth! As above, so below. As within, so without. Four stars in this place be, Combined to call the fifth to we! So mote it be."

The white light that had begun earlier brightened and was infused with the light bursting from each of the witches palms. The colors of blue, green and golden brown danced around the circle in an intricate pattern and the sudden influx of power within the circle nearly sent Caine to his knees. He glanced to the side and noticed the other males had widened their stance and were standing their ground and he did the same.

His concern about summoning Cele was melting under the evidence of the power his mate and her sisters wielded. The pride he had in that moment for his mate and her abilities awed him. His mate was bad ass and he knew they could do this. He sent that belief and his love to her through their mental link.

The females reclaimed their hands and closed their own small circle. Strong winds whipped through the clearing, sending his hair flying into his eyes. Caine felt a connection to each of the other members of the circle through their clasped hands. It amazed him how his spike in adrenaline was turned into energy for his mate and her sisters. He guessed it was the same for the other males who stood there as slack-jawed and wide-eyed as he was. A fine mist filled the circle and a buzzing built in his ears as the witches chanted a summoning spell. The words were lost on him and he closed his eyes as he struggled to keep up with translating what Suvi and her sisters were saying.

Suddenly the wind stopped and everything went silent.

Caine blinked his eyes open to see Cele crouching in the middle of the circle and the witches now wore full-leather-battle-gear from head-to-toe. He glanced down and saw that Suvi had on six-inch knee-high black boots. Of course, he smiled. The High Priestess, on the other hand, was bedraggled with her hair loose and tangled about her gaunt face. Her skin was pale and her lips chapped and bleeding. Whatever dark magic she was wielding was killing her from the inside out and he wondered if she had any idea of how bad she looked. "How dare you call me to you!" she spat indignantly.

Pema lifted her chin and addressed the angry female. "We dare because we cannot allow you to walk free with that demon's power. You have gone Dark and we will expunge that power from you."

"There is not a thing you can do to me. I am the High Priestess and you three are nothing more than lowly peasants!" Cele shrieked and tried to escape the circle. Caine tensed to move, not prepared for her to hit an invisible barrier and bounce off. He looked down and realized the witch was caught in the pentacle Isis had scribed.

"You failed to stop our power. We are now the power of three to the next fucking level. There is nothing to stop us from stripping you of all power," Isis snapped and stepped forward. The wind had picked up again and lightning flashed around them as Pema and Braeden pulled Isis back.

"What have you done with Claire?" Cele demanded, clearly not intimidated that she was surrounded by the six of them.

"The council is deciding her fate. My vote is to burn the poor thing. No one should be brought back from the dead," Suvi supplied. His mate smiled when Cele began yelling and pounding at the invisible wall. Caine was convinced the former High Priestess had finally lost her mind.

"You harm one hair on her head and I will drag you to the ninth circle of hell myself!" Cele shouted at them. "Angeica! Kadir! Come to me," Cele screamed out. She knew she was in trouble and needed assistance. Caine and the others looked around as he braced himself for the feel of dark magic. Nothing happened and he knew the moment Cele realized her allies weren't coming to her aide. Caine breathed a sigh of relief that their gamble to get Cele alone had paid off.

"What happened? Your friends aren't here to save you. Guess they aren't really your allies, after all," Isis taunted.

"You won't get away with this," Cele retorted, still trying to remain confident.

Braeden was the next one to jump into the mix. "Really? I bet we do. You're the one who will pay for what you've done. You kidnapped and tortured my son, making sure he experienced every painful moment. You slit his throat and he almost died. You are a vile creature who should be cast into hell to suffer for eternity," he roared. Caine felt a waver in their magic and wondered if the witch was finding a way through.

"I should have killed that little bastard the first time you failed me. You are weak and pathetic. One day I will find your son alone and unprotected and make him pay like my Claire has had to pay," Cele promised.

Braeden and Isis both thundered their rage to the sky. Braeden let go of the hands he was holding, breaking their circle and charging forward.

"Shit," Isis muttered and Caine felt the vibration of their magic falter. He knew the barrier was no longer surrounding Cele and she must have felt it, too, as she made a dash for the break in their circle.

Everything seemed to happen at once after that. Braeden charged Cele and plunged his hand right through her vulnerable throat. Blood spurted from the vicious wound and Cele was opening and closing her mouth, like a fish gasping for air. Braeden yelled out as he pulled his hand free and wrapped his arm around what was left of her neck.

Isis rushed forward as Braeden twisted his torso,

brutally ripping the witch's head from her neck. With one final yank, he decapitated Cele, ending her life.

Isis was sobbing and pulled him into her arms. "It's over. You and Donovan are safe now," Braeden crooned. "She will never hurt anyone again." Caine understood why Braeden had reacted the way he did. Everyone in that circle had a reason to hate Cele. She was everyone's nightmare, but it was fitting that Braeden was the one to exact revenge on Cele. His son had suffered unspeakable torture at her hands and it was his right as the boy's father.

The reality that they had eliminated this threat sank in. Cele was dead, and they were responsible. Would they face a backlash for killing Cele? It was in the witch elders' hands now, he supposed. He prayed to the Goddess they would see it as justified.

Suvi paced the meeting room at Cailleach Academy. The image of Braeden ripping Cele's head from her shoulders had haunted her for two days. They had barely slept from worrying that Braeden may be put to death for killing the High Priestess. Not that any of them believed he should be punished for his actions, but that didn't mean the elders would agree. Suvi laid her hands on top of Caine's where they were wrapped around her stomach. Having him close brought comfort and calmed her frayed nerves.

The loud thump of heavy footsteps echoed from the hall. They were coming to give the verdict. Suddenly, Suvi felt as if she may be sick. She crossed to Isis and pulled her into a hug. If anyone knew how her sister felt, she did. She recalled, all too well, how it had felt to have Caine facing a death sentence. Pema came up on Isis' other side and they stood as a unit with their mates close behind.

Zander strode into the room first, his face a blank mask. Behind him followed the rest of the Dark Alliance council. She was unable to read their faces either. Ezra, Beatrice, and Livia strode in behind the males. The trio of elder witches weren't what you'd think of when you thought elders. Considering they were centuries old, they all appeared to be young, beautiful females in their early thirties. Suvi's nerves were twisted in knots and she held her breath, waiting in anticipation.

Zander fastened his eyes on Braeden. "First, lad, I want to thank you for eliminating a threat to the realm. No' only had this witch harmed our precious *bairns*, she had turned evil and partnered with Kadir. Had she succeeded in her plans, nothing on earth would be safe."

Beatrice cleared her throat and stepped forward. "Normally, the punishment for killing a High Priestess is death, but not in this instance. You did what any male would do to protect his Fated Mate and son. The realm is blessed to have you amongst its ranks and we plan to keep it that way for centuries to come." Suvi let out the breath she had been holding and felt Isis' relief wash over her, it was that enormous.

Zander briefly looked around the room and then back at their group. "We didna only discuss the situation involving Cele's death. We also discussed the three of you," he relayed, nodding to Suvi and her sisters in turn. His words set the butterflies in Suvi's stomach in motion once again. What was he talking about?

Ezra joined the conversation. "As you know, leadership in the realm is passed down in families. We are faced with an unprecedented situation right now. Cele's only child was

Claire who is deceased and there are no other members of her line. After much debate, we feel that there isn't one person appropriate to take on the role. The decision had been made to appoint the three of you to the positions of High Priestesses."

Suvi's mouth dropped open. No way had she heard her correctly. She must have misunderstood. How could they appoint all three of them? Sure, she had grown up being the object of the prophecy and had even recently realized that she was indeed destined to reform witchcraft as they knew it, but she never would have imagined being appointed at such a young age. She was speechless at the opportunity being offered to them. A million thoughts raced through her mind, from how they could bring witchcraft into the modern day, to not wanting any part of this. They were happy running Black Moon Sabbat, after all. Why rock the boat?

Livia cleared her throat and stepped next to Zander. "From the moment you were born, each one of us knew you were our future. We need you to take over this great institution and educate our young." For the third time in a matter of minutes Suvi was stunned. They expected them to run the Academy *and* educate their young? And, they weren't afraid they would corrupt them?

Zander chuckled at her reaction. "'Tis a lot to take in, but before you answer, take time and think it over. Not only do the witches need you, the Dark Alliance council needs you. Females are being kidnapped by Kadir and we could use your particular talents in helping us rescue them."

The rush of adrenaline barreled through Suvi. She looked at her sisters and they shared a knowing smile. She knew there would be no discussion necessary.

"Watch this, mom," Donovan called out and then tore across the deck at high speed and jumped into the pool. Water splashed out and soaked the deck around them. Suvi turned and smiled at her nephew.

"That's great, honey," Isis called back before returning to their discussion. They had been planning the rescue of the females from Kadir's lair for hours now and everyone was tired.

She grabbed Caine's hand and gave it a squeeze. "Are you sure it's safe to go in? You said you had a premonition that we shouldn't attempt a rescue yet," she asked Zander's mate, Elsie.

"A week ago, I did have that premonition, but this morning I had a new one. This one was more urgent, indicating that we will lose one of our own if we don't go in soon," Elsie replied.

"Did you see what we will face?" Pema asked.

"I saw hellhounds and fury demons, as well as skirm. Kadir and Azazel weren't part of the premonition, but we can't assume that means they won't be there." Elsie looked surprisingly eager, given that she was fairly new to her role in the Tehrex Realm. Suvi guessed the Queen had been fraught with worry about these females for the past week.

"You will be our rear guard of sorts," Zander went on to explain. "Aside from Ronan, you are no' trained in combat. We need you there to cast a spell that will prohibit the archdemons from teleporting away from the scene. I want to end this once and for all. No' that Lucifer willna simply send more to replace them, but it will give us a reprieve."

"I'm not sure if our spell would stop the archdemons, but we can sure try," Pema agreed.

Donovan came running to the table with a big bullfrog in his hands. "Mom, do you have a jar? I want to keep it. I named him Fred. Isn't he cool?"

Suvi couldn't help but burst into laughter at that. She caught her sisters' knowing gazes and they, too, fell into a fit of hysterics. "Sure, honey. I have a jar in the house, but *she* already has a name. Just call her Plain Paula."

EXCERPT FROM SCARRED WARRIOR, DARK WARRIOR ALLIANCE BOOK 7

Gerrick paced another circuit through the warriors milling around, anxious as hell to get the show on the road. "I say we go in guns blazing, right now. And, I know we don't use guns, Mack, so don't go being a smart ass," he snarled at the female who hadn't actually said anything. His muscles twitched in his arms and he reached for his weapons. Adrenaline dumped into his system, making his heart race.

Mack, Prince Kyran's Fated Mate, threw up her hands. "Don't pick on me, Oscar the Grouch. I'm ready to get in there, too. I'm the one who found them, remember?"

Before Mack mated Kyran and became an intricate part of their group, she stumbled upon the archdemon's lair and discovered where he was holding several females prisoner. Gerrick and his fellow warriors had been searching ceaselessly, night and day for the location of the missing females, but were unsuccessful. It had been a source of frustration for him that he hadn't been able to protect the females from harm. It was his duty as a Dark Warrior to protect the innocent from the demons and their minions.

Zander placed his hand on Gerrick's shoulder, stopping him mid-stride. "Patience. We canna go in without setting up the barriers. Pema, Isis and Suvi are doing their part now and you and Jace are up next. Focus on that."

Gerrick took a deep breath, knowing the Vampire King was right, but it was difficult when his blood was calling for him to take action. It was a painful compulsion that was impossible to ignore, but there was no mistaking the command in Zander's tone. Gerrick took several more deep breaths, trying to settle his anxiousness and concentrate on what he needed to do next.

Gerrick paused next to Jace and pulled his staff out of its magical pocket of space in the Goddess' realm. Immediately, he felt the additional power surge through his limbs. The seven-foot, gnarled, basswood pole was given to him by his father when he became an adult and his thumb went unerringly to the small silver pendant wrapped around the leather grip. Sorrow and rage spiked, making it difficult to focus. Not willing to let himself get mired in the past, he checked his surroundings in the dark parking lot.

Gerrick wasn't comfortable with the number of humans in the area. They were about to stir the hornet's nest and he didn't want innocent bystanders harmed because they happened to be in the wrong place at the wrong time. It went against his warrior's oath, but there was nothing they could do about it since Kadir had set up shop in the middle of downtown Seattle.

He glanced around the corner of the brick building and braced himself against the bitter wind and chilling rain. He watched a human male hurry from a shop and make his way in their direction. Gerrick quickly muttered a spell, sending the male into a nearby coffee chop, or at least, Gerrick thought it was a coffee shop. The old-fashioned architecture and brickwork of the businesses in Pioneer Square were all so similar it was hard to tell them apart. He shrugged figuring the human was safe enough.

"This is a much bigger area than we have ever covered before, Zander," Pema piped up a few seconds later. "There are so many exits to consider. I'm not sure we can do this." Gerrick turned around and saw that the witch triplets were holding hands and each of their mates was touching their shoulders. He watched the vibrant pinks and red lights of their magic swirl around their bodies. To his sensitive sorcerer's vision it was bright, almost blinding.

He had faith the witches could manage to spell. After all, the freshly-crowned High Priestesses were by far the most powerful witches in the Tehrex Realm and were the most recent additions to the Dark Alliance Council.

Zander caught his attention as he slid his *sgian dubh* into the sheath around his waist. Zander's presence was vast and it had nothing to do with the fact that he was a king. It was his inherent power and confidence. Gerrick was surrounded by the most powerful men in the realm, but none of them held a candle to Zander. The thing that made him so extraordinary was that he shared this power and confidence with those around him. "I know this is a large area and 'tis going to be impossible to include all possible exits. Cover as many as you can, but leave the ones that lead to the water open. The water will help hem them in. The goal is to keep the demons from fleeing, but, first and foremost, we canna allow feral skirm to get out and attack humans."

Music blared into the night as the door to a bar on Yesler Street opened and several humans stumbled out. Collectively, the group of supernaturals tensed, and no one uttered a word.

"It would be nice if you had the power to order everyone out of the area, Zander," Gerrick mumbled. He took a deep breath to calm his nerves and took in a lungful of acrid urine with a backdrop of briny sea. It was enough to make him gag and nearly lose his dinner.

"You guys are overthinking this," Mack piped up. "It's two a.m. and any people who are walking around right now are probably drunk and certainly not paying attention to us. Besides, we aren't near a residential area. Just minimize the risk these bastards will pose and let's get in there." Gerrick liked the feisty female and smiled when he saw her latest t-shirt that said 'I love my bloodsucker.' She was always referring to her mate as a bloodsucker, or leech, or some other smartass term and Gerrick had no doubt that Kyran must have given her the tee.

"Make sure to stay by my side, Firecracker. I doona want you running in their thinking you can take on the whole lair. You may be immortal now, but you're no' invincible," Kyran told her, tugging on a strand of her spiky, black hair. The vampire prince had undergone a drastic attitude change when he had been stuck in the dragon realm with his mate, and was no longer the unhappy, distant warrior that he used to be. Gerrick acknowledged the new Kyran was definitely a change for the better.

"Ok, we're done. You guys are up." Pema's voice jolted Gerrick's thoughts, making his pulse leap. They were one step closer to going in and it was none too soon.

"Thanks," Gerrick nodded and checked to make sure Jace was ready. Jace was the healer of their group, but also a kick-ass fighter and the most powerful sorcerer in the realm and Gerrick was glad to have the male fighting by his side.

Jace met his gaze and they began chanting in the old language.

Green, blue and purple lights of Jace and Gerrick's magic were added to the reds and pinks of the witches. Gerrick locked in on the ten-block boundary the witches had cast around Pioneer Square and wove his enchantments with theirs. When the last word of the spell left his lips, he was sweating and breathing hard, but the flash of white light signaled that they had been successful.

Gerrick turned to Zander, "It's done, Liege," he informed. Sorcerers had the ability to see magic whereas the other supernaturals could only feel it. Only the sorcerers had seen the flash of white indicating the spell was completed.

Zander shifted his stance, his authoritative tone grabbing everyone's attention. "Hayden, take your shifters and wait by your entrance. Kyran, take your group to your spot. The rest of you, follow me. Everyone sync the time, we enter in five. Remember, our mission here is to get in and rescue the females and take oot the archdemons if we can."

"Stay alert," Gerrick told the witches and their mates, who would all be remaining behind. "The females may be feral and try to escape. We have to be prepared for the worst case scenarios." He shuddered to think about what horrors they had been suffering at the hands of such evil. It hadn't sat well with him to delay the rescue after Elsie had her premonition, but they all knew better than to dismiss the warning so they had waited.

He adjusted his black leather jacket and returned his staff, wishing he'd chosen a heavier coat since the weather was decidedly cold in December in Seattle, especially so close to the water. But leather offered more protection against knives and teeth, so everyone was dressed in leather from head to toe.

"What do we do if we encounter them?" Suvi asked, pursing her lips and stomping her impossibly high heels on the pavement. How the witch managed to stand, much less run or fight, was a mystery to him, but she didn't seem fazed by them one bit.

"Contain them, but doona harm them unless there is no choice. Jessie is proof that females are no' mindless like male skirm. We are here to help them," Zander replied, echoing Gerrick's thoughts. "Alright, move oot."

Gerrick jumped into motion behind Kyran and Mack. Their group silently made their way to a stairwell that led down to the Underground. The area wasn't ideal to face demons and skirm. They were entering the burned remains of Seattle and Gerrick had no doubt it wasn't the most stable of areas, especially when considering a battle.

Gerrick recalled what Seattle was like before the great Fire of 1889. There were horse-drawn carriages and dirt roads, and there wasn't this sense of urgency to get from one place to the next. It was vastly different from the city today. Then again, life in general back then was very different without modern technology. Gerrick enjoyed the easier way of life, but wouldn't want to give up his cell phone and the Internet. Having information at the tips of his fingers was invaluable to their work.

The group made their way down weathered cement steps and Kyran paused at the bottom when Mack put her hand on his arm. "Don't get dead, bloodsucker," the inked female muttered.

Kyran smiled broadly and stroked her pink cheek with one finger. "Doona do something stupid, like taking on Kadir." Gerrick watched as Mack smiled wryly and nodded.

This was their version of 'I love you.' They weren't the mushy type of couple and Gerrick was glad of that. The last thing he needed was to have it rubbed in his face of what he would never have.

Gerrick looked back over his shoulder and took stock of their group. Aside from himself, Mack, and Kyran, there was Rhys and the New Orleans Dark Warriors. Rhys was Gerrick's patrol partner. Like Gerrick, Rhys lived at Zeum with the Seattle Dark Warriors. He was the jokester of their group, always pulling practical jokes on everyone, but Gerrick knew there was more lurking beneath the surface with Rhys.

The sound of metal screeching caught his attention as Kyran forced the door open and made his way into the building. The second the door fully opened the scent of mold and stale air hit him. Underlying it he caught hints of rodents, feces, urine and skirm. As they descended a flight of stairs, weathered cement gave way to newer wooden ones. The human authorities were often replacing rotted sections of the underground and Gerrick wondered why the humans hadn't run into the demons before now. Kadir must be expending a lot of energy to keep his lair hidden.

The next section was very narrow, and they had to go single file. He noted the brick of the previous buildings was wearing away, and in need of repair. They passed several unrecognizable businesses, and had to climb over timber and other debris. What struck him as odd were the many old toilets and it was beyond him that humans left this stuff to rot down here.

Gerrick cocked his ears and heard noise in the distance and pointed in the direction they needed to travel. Aison, one of the New Orleans Dark Warriors, jumped over an old, faded sofa and disturbed a family of rats. Gerrick had to hold back his laugh when the warrior did a little jig to avoid the scurrying rodents.

It was a maze down there and difficult to maneuver at times, which were definitely not ideal fighting conditions. There was so much flammable material all around them that Gerrick worried they would spark the next devastating Seattle fire when they killed the skirm. Unfortunately, Gerrick didn't see a way around using titanium blades on the skirm since it was the easiest way to kill them.

The scent of brimstone and death heightened, telling him they were close. Kyran held up his hand and they all stopped.

"The females are around the corner and down the hall," Mack whispered.

Gerrick cast a silencing spell over their group and they crept on silent feet around the corner and discovered they were near the old steam baths. It was far less cluttered and it was obvious someone had cleared out most of the rubble, converting the space into living quarters.

Kyran opened the door and flattened against the wall, with the rest of them following suit. Gerrick wanted to laugh at what he imagined was a comical sight with nine large males standing flat against the wall as if pinned there.

Kyran poked his head around and his stance relaxed. They unfolded from the wall and Gerrick noticed that the business they were entering used to be an apothecary, at least according to the chipping paint on the dirt-encrusted window. Several walls had been knocked down to create one large space and the room was empty except for a large circular cage in the middle.

A crash suddenly sounded and Mack took off running, Kyran cursing as he chased after her. The rest of them were in motion a second later and they all came to a sudden halt inside a space that was dark, musty and crowded with cages. These cages were much smaller compared to the last one they saw, and were all full of females. Gerrick stumbled as the stench nearly bowled him over. There were so many different odors competing for dominance it was dizzying. Gerrick detected rotting flesh, feces, urine, and brimstone, as well as, moldy, charred fabric and wood. He glanced around and saw a pile of corpses in the corner in various stages of decomposition and shuddered in revulsion. Those poor beings deserved better than to be tossed aside like garbage.

Gerrick didn't have time to stop and consider anything further as the room was in the midst of a battle between demons and Zander's group. Gerrick recognized the hellhounds from a previous battle at Woodland Park, and bit back a curse. They were vicious beasts and relentless in their pursuit. There were also fury demons and large slimy green demons. He needed to try and put a muzzle on his anger, but the sight before him was infuriating. The last thing he wanted was to feed the fury demons power.

Before he could react, a slavering dog the size of a horse charged into him, knocking him down. He jumped up, weapons in hand and slashed the dog's snout. A high-pitched whine and shake of the head was all the injury earned Gerrick, but it was enough for him to sever the tendon on one of its front paws. Unfortunately, the beast wasn't slowed down on three legs. It glared at him through glowing red eyes, the desire to kill clearly expressed.

Completely focused on his target, Gerrick danced out of the next charge. He cursed when he wasn't fast enough to avoid its canines. When the hound's teeth didn't break through his leather, Gerrick was glad he hadn't gone with the warmer clothing.

Taking the offensive, Gerrick charged the demon and wrapped his arms around its thick neck. He head-butted the beast when it snapped at his face, keeping a firm grip on the animal. Gerrick lifted his weapon, opening himself up to the beast. He brought down his *sgian dubh* and cut into slick, black skin while canines clamped down on his shoulder and gnawed, slowly working their way through the leather.

Grimacing, Gerrick never let up and plunged his knife into the hellhound, trying to hit its heart. He could feel the dog moving them across the floor until metal bars of a cage instead scraped against his back. Finally, after several minutes his weapon hit its mark and the hellhound let out a screech that sounded a lot like tires skidding on asphalt and went still in his embrace. Gerrick gave one last twist of the blade, ensuring the beast was dead. He let go and kicked the hound away.

Gerrick jumped when a hand touched his injured shoulder. Panting and out of breath, Gerrick turned and his heart stopped for several beats when he caught sight of the female in the cage. She was stark naked. Her neck and shoulder had thick scars from obvious bite marks and she was bruised from head to toe. And she was filthy. Her hair was tangled mess and he thought it may be red, but it was hard to tell with how dirty it was. However, it was her eyes that stopped him cold. Their jade green depths were haunted, and, for some reason, very familiar.

They had obviously found the female prisoners and this one couldn't be more of a mess, but she had his body reacting with a ferocity that rocked him. It was the absolute worst time to be turned on and attracted to a female. It was even worse given the trauma this particular female had obviously suffered, but neither common sense nor the life and death fight he was engaged in stopped him from wanting this female beyond reason. He couldn't think straight, he was so enthralled.

"Behind you!" the female shouted, breaking the spell.

SHAE WAS dumb-founded that the Vampire King and his Dark Warriors had come to rescue them. She blinked, wondering if it was a trick of the infrared vision she'd inherited along with the bloodlust. She knew something was happening when countless skirm and demons rushed into the room where she had been held prisoner. Seconds later her prayers were answered with the influx of warriors. She had prayed and begged to be set free or killed and now she couldn't stop the hope and joy that sparked at the sight before her.

Tears brimmed in her eyes when she realized she was finally going to get out of that cage, one way or another.

She stared at the warrior with the gaze that was cold as ice. He had fought the hellhound like a male who had nothing to lose, charging the fiend and wrapping his muscular arms around the beast. It was a bloody and unreal sight, but now that she looked into his eyes, she saw a male lost, broken, and alone. It reflected how she felt inside. She noticed that he was scarred like her, too. The left side of his face had a scar from his temple to his neck, but the sight didn't detract from his good looks. It just made him look dangerous...and delicious.

She caught movement out of the corner of her eye. "Behind you," she warned.

Before she blinked, he swiveled and his blade found purchase in the chest of the approaching skirm. He wasted no time getting right back into the fight. He was a thing of beauty as he killed enemy after enemy, never tiring while blood poured from his shoulder. She smelled his blood and looked down to see it coated her fingers and bloodlust had her close to licking every drop from her skin.

A skirm banged into her cage, distracting her wicked thoughts, and she reached through and grabbed hold of its head. She twisted and pulled and tugged until the body fell at her feet. She lifted her head and glanced into stunned, whiskey eyes. "You came back for us. I thought you were dead," Shae muttered.

"You bet your ass I came back. I'd have been here sooner, but I had a detour in Khoth. We are getting you out of here...just as soon...as we can." The last was said while the female battled a skirm who had come up behind her. She was fierce and fought like the wind. And, Shae noted, she wasn't human anymore. She had mated to one of the vampire royal family as the Tarakesh family mark inked below her left ear caught her eye. Shae hadn't seen the mystical mate mark the last time she had seen the female and wondered if her prompting the search for the King brought her to her Fated Mate.

Shae knew the tales about mate marks, and how and when they appeared. For human mates, the mate mark always appeared below the left ear, and was a mystical mark until the mating was completed. At this point it became inked into the skin, never to be removed. Aside from those of her parents and grandparents, she had never actually seen a mate mark, thanks to a seven-century long mating curse. The curse had been lifted recently and Fated Mates were being blessed once again.

Prince Kyran worked his way next to the female and took care of the fury demon targeting his mate. "I see you've managed to find trouble, Firecracker."

"No more than usual. What the hell are those nasty things?" the female asked. Shae looked over to see several pus demons had joined the fight. Shae recalled fighting one of those bastards in the cage not long ago. The slime they left in their wake made battle challenging as was evidenced when one of the Dark Warriors skidded and slammed into a wall. The brittle boards of the wall rattled, but held up as he pushed into a leap and sliced his knife through the demons throat. Green pus oozed from the wound and the smell it emitted was noxious. It didn't faze Shae like it did the warriors who visibly gagged, but she had to agree it was vile.

Her scarred warrior was embroiled in his own fight with one of the four-armed pus demons. She had no idea why her mind insisted on claiming this stranger, but it did, none-theless. He was caught by two of the demon's arms while the other two reached for his head. Blue-eyes flashed and he elbowed the demon in the gut in an attempt to free himself. Shae watched as his elbow sunk ineffectively into the fleshy body.

"The groin!" she shouted, trying to get his attention. "Go for the groin."

Ice-cold eyes turned on her and he inclined his head in acknowledgment. A second later, the demon bellowed and her warrior fell to the ground, and without wasting time, proceeded to hack its head off. He was a fearless champion, and made her blood boil hotter than a fresh pot of coffee.

Another warrior cried out as he was caught in four slimy arms. Her warrior leapt through the air and buried his blade in the top of that demon's head as he sailed over it. He landed easily on his feet and swiveled to face a skirm coming up from behind. The first warrior took care of the pus demon while her warrior fought on. Within no time, both males were standing there panting, having vanquished their foes for the time being.

"Thanks, Gerrick." Shae made a mental note that her blue-eyed, scarred warrior was named Gerrick.

"No problem, Caell."

The two warriors turned and raised their weapons, ready to continue, but there were no more enemies in their immediate area. Shae could hear more heading their way. "Get us out, now. Hurry, there are more coming," Shae pleaded with the female who had brought salvation back with her.

"My name is Mack, and it will be my pleasure to finally make good on my promise." Mack lifted her foot to kick the lock while others worked on the remaining cages, but the prince was there before her foot landed.

"I had that, bloodsucker," Mack complained.

"I know you did," he replied as Shae was finally freed. Without thought, she was rushing Mack and enveloping her in a tight hug.

"I'm Shae and I owe you my life." It had been countless weeks, maybe months, of torture, rape and fighting and now she was out of that cage. They may not be in the clear yet, but she wasn't ever going back into that cage. She'd die first. "Saying thank you isn't enough for what you've given us. If you ever need anything don't hesitate to call on me."

"Save that for later. Do you know a fast way out of here? The way we came in is too far from here," Mack said, cutting her off and reached into her backpack.

"I have no idea. I was teleported into this room."

Mack handed her a pile of clothes and Shae shook her head. "Give them to Cami. She needs them more." She glanced over at the human who was shaking from the terror. She wasn't so human anymore. The frail female had been in their midst the shortest amount of time, but was by far the most traumatized.

"We will have to go back the way we came then. Come on, we better get out of here now," Gerrick barked. Even clipped and terse, his voice was a balm to her soul, and damned if her body wasn't responding, as well. It was both reassuring and deeply disturbing that the horrors she had suffered hadn't left her dead inside. Shae turned and started for the entrance, ready to leave this part of her life behind her.

AUTHOR'S NOTE

Authors' Note

With new digital download trends, authors rely on readers to spread the word more than ever. Here are some ways to help us.

Leave a review! Every author asks their readers to take five minutes and let others know how much you enjoyed their work. Here's the reason why. Reviews help your favorite authors to become visible. It's simple and easy to do. If you are a Kindle user turn to the last page and leave a review before you close your book. For other retailers, just visit their online site and leave a brief review.

Don't forget to visit our website: www.trimandjulka.com and sign up for our newsletter, which is jam-packed with exciting news and monthly giveaways. Also, be sure to visit and like our Facebook page https://www.facebook.com/TrimAndJulka to see our daily themes, including hot guys, drink recipes and book teasers.

Trust your journey and remember that the future is yours and it's filled with endless possibilities!

DREAM BIG!
XOXO,
Brenda & Tami

OTHER WORKS BY TRIM AND JULKA

OTHER WORKS BY TRIM AND JULKA

The Dark Warrior Alliance

OTHER WORKS BY TRIM AND JULKA

The Rowan Sisters' Trilogy

NEWSLETTER SIGNUP

Don't miss out!
Click the button below and you can sign up to receive emails from Trim and Julka about new releases, fantastic giveaways, and their latest hand made jewelry. There's no charge and no obligation.

Printed in Great Britain
by Amazon

48448917R00090